ROMEO

&

JULIET

Translated for Gen Z

Shakespeare for Gen Z

ROMEO & JULIET

Translated for Gen Z

Published by

Shakespeare for Gen Z

Book Cover by: Muhammad Waqas

First edition: 2024

ISBN: 9798876963055

ROMEO

&

JULIET

Translated for Gen Z

'Our doubts are traitors and make us lose the good we oft might win, by fearing to attempt.' - William Shakespeare, Measure for Measure, Act I Scene IV.

Dedicated to Gen Z, your energy, creativity, and unique way of viewing the world have inspired a new lens through which to experience this classic tale.

Introduction

This translation of Romeo and Juliet is a true testament to the power of storytelling and its ability to span generations. The language of Shakespeare's work can seem to some as distant as the era in which it was written. We aim to close this gap. Here, we take this classic tale of love, fate, and conflict and reintroduce it in the vibrant and hilarious language of Gen Z. I hope you thoroughly enjoy reading this testament to the power of storytelling, and every generation having its own story to tell.

- Shakespeare for Gen Z

ROMEO

&

JULIET

ACT ONE

ACT TWO

ACT THREE

ACT FOUR

ACT FIVE

CHARACTERS

Romeo - This guy's the main dude, 16 and all in his feels. Starts off moping over Rosaline, then goes full send for Juliet. He's a total snack, smart, a true simp with heavy emotions.

Juliet - She's 13, the lead chick. Straight-up gorgeous and gets all the butterflies for Romeo. She's the definition of 'pure' but quickly changes her status for her bae, Romeo.

Mercutio - Romeo's squadmate, the king of wild banter. He's the guy with the wild inappropriate jokes, big on honor and respect.

Tybalt - Juliet's cuz. He's got zero chill, always down to throw hands, and keeps that grudge against the Montagues on simmer.

Benvolio - Romeo's cuz and voice of reason. Chill vibes only, tries to keep the peace, and drops some legit wisdom.

Friar Laurence - The holy man in Romeo's corner. Big on the wise talks, solid intentions, and the unofficial life coach for R&J when stuff gets real.

Capulet - Juliet's dad and the boss of the Capulet household. He really loves his daughter but doesn't really get her. He's usually cool but can totally lose it if things don't go his way, especially when it comes to setting Juliet up with Paris.

Lady Capulet - Juliet's mama, all about arranging that power couple with Paris. She keeps it one hundred with formality and delegates the mom duties to the nurse.

Paris - The guy with the family ties to the prince, shooting his shot with Juliet. He's got the looks, stacks, and is the guy who's 'good on paper', but his rizz? Not so much.

Prince Escalus - The guy running Verona, big on law and order, super focused on keeping things chill in the city.

Montague - Romeo's dad, lowkey stressed about his son's sadboi phase.

Lady Montague - Romeo's mom, who's heart can't even when Romeo gets the ban hammer from Verona.

Friar John - This Franciscan friar gets the one job to DM Romeo about Juliet's fake-out death, but gets stuck in a quarantine sitch and totally drops the ball. Ghosted by fate, our boy Romeo never gets the memo.

Balthasar - Romeo's ride-or-die homie. He hits Romeo with the fake news of Juliet's death, not knowing it's all just a big misunderstanding.

Sampson and Gregory - They're down for their squad and start the whole drama by beefing with the Montague boys right off the bat.

The Apothecary - The dude in Mantua running a pharmacy that's only got like, two stars. He's so broke he puts cash over conscience and sells Romeo the ultimate sleep aid.

Rosaline - The O.G. crush of Romeo who never steps on stage but is like this invisible influencer everyone says is a total badie. She's playing life on hard mode with a vow of chastity.

The Chorus - This one's the voiceover pro, breaking down the plot and the feels of the play, kind of like a hype man setting the scene for us.

ROMEO

&

JULIET

Translated for Gen Z

Shakespeare for Gen Z

THE PROLOGUE

*(Enter **Chorus**)*

CHORUS

Two households, both alike in dignity, in fair Verona, where we lay our scene, from ancient grudge break to new mutiny, where civil blood makes civil hands unclean. From forth the fatal loins of these two foes a pair of star-crossed lovers take their life; whose misadventure piteous overthrows doth with their death bury their parents' strife. The fearful passage of their death-marked love, and the continuance of their parents' rage, which, but their children's end, nought could remove, is now the two hours' traffic of our stage; The which if you with patient ears attend, what here shall miss, our toil shall strive to mend.

(Exit)

THE PROLOGUE

*(Enter **Chorus**)*

CHORUS

Two households, both with plenty clout, in fair Verona, where we spill this tea, from ancient beef break to new mutiny. Where civil bros stain their hands in blood. Of these two fams, spawn a pair of star-crossed lovers who straight-up unalive themselves. Their tragic vibe as they leave the chat, totally cancels the family drama, and squashes the beef. For the span of two hours' time, we shall gaze upon this tale of forbidden love, and wrath of bad boomer blood, which naught but their offspring's canceling could nerf. So chill, and vibe with us as we spill this tea in the tongue of Gen Z.

(Exit)

ACT ONE

SCENE ONE

*(Enter **Sampson** and **Gregory**, of the house of Capulet, armed with swords and bucklers)*

SAMPSON

Gregory, o' my word, we'll not carry coals.

GREGORY

No, for then we should be colliers.

SAMPSON

I mean, an we be in choler, we'll draw.

GREGORY

Ay, while you live, draw your neck out o' the collar.

SAMPSON

I strike quickly, being moved.

ACT ONE

SCENE ONE

*(**Sampson** and **Gregory**, enter reppin' Capulet colors)*

SAMPSON

Aye fam, let's not let them Montagues catch us slippin'. We can't be taking any Ls.

GREGORY

*(Making fun of **Sampson**)* Nay, for are we not built different?

SAMPSON

Facts! If any Montague bros press us, be ready to throw hands.

GREGORY

Why you always gotta feel some type of way, Sampson? Always trying to catch the smoke.

SAMPSON

Bet, I'll turn fierce if they doin' too much!

GREGORY

But thou art not quickly moved to strike.

SAMPSON

A dog of the house of Montague moves me.

GREGORY

To move is to stir; and to be valiant is to stand: therefore, if thou art moved, thou runn'st away.

SAMPSON

A dog of that house shall move me to stand: I will take the wall of any man or maid of Montague's.

GREGORY

That shows thee a weak slave; for the weakest goes to the wall.

SAMPSON

True; and therefore women, being the weaker vessels, are ever thrust to the wall: therefore I will push Montague's men from the wall, and thrust his maids to the wall.

GREGORY

Bro, you are doing the most rn.

SAMPSON

On God, if a Montague bro wants to act out...

GREGORY

You might ghost' em with an Irish goodbye?

SAMPSON

You play too much. If an opp gets me heated, they gonna catch
the smoke. If I clock one on the street, 'tis I who'll stand tall while
they shall be the ones duckin' me.

GREGORY

Bruh, if you seek "problems not peace, problems always" surely,
you shall find yourself catching many Ls.

SAMPSON

Yae, facts. Tis problems I seek always! Yet I shall feast and leave
no crumbs.

GREGORY

The quarrel is between our masters and us their men.

SAMPSON

'Tis all one, I will show myself a tyrant: when I have fought with the men, I will be cruel with the maids, and cut off their heads.

GREGORY

The heads of the maids?

SAMPSON

Ay, the heads of the maids, or their maidenheads; take it in what sense thou wilt.

GREGORY

They must take it in sense that feel it.

SAMPSON

Me they shall feel while I am able to stand: and 'tis known I am a pretty piece of flesh.

GREGORY

Understand the assignment, fam! We are merely hype men for
this ancient 1v1.

SAMPSON

Ayo, check this out, after I throw hands with the fellows, I'll rizz
up their maidens aye, go for the neck, ya feel?

GREGORY

Oh, word? Go for the neck? Or are you speaking of other
endeavors?

SAMPSON

Take that however you want, fam.

GREGORY

On God, you will be lucky if you even get friendzoned.

SAMPSON

Bruh, they cant help themselves! I got that main character
energy.

GREGORY

'Tis well thou art not fish; if thou hadst, thou hadst been poor John. Draw thy tool! here comes two of the house of the Montagues.

*(Enter **Abram** and another Montague)*

SAMPSON

My naked weapon is out: quarrel, I will back thee.

GREGORY

How! turn thy back and run?

SAMPSON

Fear me not.

GREGORY

No, marry; I fear thee!

SAMPSON

Let us take the law of our sides; let them begin.

GREGORY

I will frown as I pass by, and let them take it as they list.

GREGORY

Do inform me when that update drops. Awe, snap! Here we go again. Here come some Montegues.

*(Enter **Abram** and another Montague)*

SAMPSON

Aye, I'm prepared to clutch.

GREGORY

Will you clutch? Or will you ghost me in my hour of need?

SAMPSON

Chill bruh, let me cook.

GREGORY

High-key, you better match my energy.

SAMPSON

Say less, but let them be the first to start throwing hands.

GREGORY

Aye, I shall cast the side eye. Me personally, I would not let that slide.

SAMPSON

Nay, as they dare. I will bite my thumb at them; which is a
disgrace to them, if they bear it.

ABRAM

Do you bite your thumb at us, sir?

SAMPSON

I do bite my thumb, sir.

ABRAM

Do you bite your thumb at us, sir?

SAMPSON

(Aside to **Gregory***)* Is the law of our side, if I say ay?

GREGORY

No.

SAMPSON

No, sir, I do not bite my thumb at you, sir, but I bite my thumb.

GREGORY

Do you quarrel, sir?

SAMPSON

Trust, this will live rent free in their head. *(He doth flip the bird)*

ABRAM

Holdup, did you just flip me off?

SAMPSON

Nay, 'twas but an emote.

ABRAM

Oh, I thought maybe you were looking for trouble.

SAMPSON

*(In a hushed voice to **Gregory**)* Is it within the king's law to flex at this juncture?

GREGORY

*(In a hushed voice to **Sampson**)* Chill bro, we'll be caught in 4k.

SAMPSON

Nay Abram, the gesture was not for you.

GREGORY

Do you seek these hands, or what?

ABRAM

Quarrel sir! no, sir.

SAMPSON

If you do, sir, I am for you: I serve as good a man as you.

ABRAM

No better.

SAMPSON

Well, sir.

*(Here enters **Benvolio** with stealth)*

GREGORY

Say 'better:' here comes one of my master's kinsmen.

SAMPSON

Yes, better, sir.

ABRAM

You lie.

ABRAM

Nay, fam.

SAMPSON

Good sir, if thou desires to throw hands, I stand ready. My lord too ranks amongst top G's.

ABRAM

Yet he ranks not as the "top G," I bet.

SAMPSON

Bet.

*(Here enters **Benvolio** with stealth)*

GREGORY

(*In a soft tone to **Sampson***) Bro, claim his lord to be mid.

SAMPSON

(*To **Abram***) Yo, your lord ain't but a "Mid G".

ABRAM

That's cap.

SAMPSON

Draw, if you be men. Gregory, remember thy swashing blow.

(They fight)

BENVOLIO

Part, fools! Put up your swords; you know not what you do. Beats down their swords.

*(Enter **Tybalt**)*

TYBALT

What, art thou drawn among these heartless hinds? Turn thee, Benvolio, look upon thy death.

BENVOLIO

I do but keep the peace: put up thy sword, or manage it to part these men with me.

TYBALT

What, drawn, and talk of peace! I hate the word, as I hate hell, all Montagues, and thee: have at thee, coward!

(They fight)

SAMPSON

Bust out that blade if you're doing it for the plot. "Ayo, Greg, never back down, never what?"

(The conflict escalates, and they draw swords)

BENVOLIO

(Unsheathing his sword) Y'all doin too much! Sheath your irons, you feral ones!

*(**Tybalt** spawns)*

TYBALT

Oh, word? You engage with these simps? Turn then, Benvolio, so I can clap those cheeks!

BENVOLIO

This quarrel doesn't need to escalate, fam! Be a real one and uphold the peace!

TYBALT

Nah, you're trippin' brandishing your steel, speaking of peace! Such math ain't mathin', prepare to catch this L!

*(**Benvolio** and **Tybalt** start throwing hands)*

(Enter, several of both houses, who join the fray; then enter Citizens, with clubs)

CITIZENS

Clubs, bills, and partisans! strike! beat them down! Down with the Capulets! down with the Montagues!

*(Enter **Capulet** in his gown, and **Lady Capulet**)*

CAPULET

What noise is this? Give me my long sword, ho!

LADY CAPULET

A crutch, a crutch! why call you for a sword?

*(Enter **Montegue** and **Lady Montegue**)*

CAPULET

My sword, I say! Old Montague is come, and flourishes his blade in spite of me.

MONTAGUE

Thou villain Capulet,--Hold me not, let me go.

(Enter armed citizens, much aggrieved for they were down bad)

CITIZENS

Cancel the Capulets! Cancel the Montagues!

*(**Capulet** enters, with his ride or die, **Lady Capulet**)*

CAPULET

Fetch me my sword, babygirl!

LADY CAPULET

Bruh, you are past the age of beekeeping, chill!

*(**Montague** arrives, sword drawn, with **Lady Montague**)*

CAPULET

Why gatekeep my blade from me? Ol' Montague's out here flexing his steel.

MONTAGUE

You're such a Karen, Capulet! *(As **Lady Montague** restrains him)* Release me, so I can go off!

LADY MONTAGUE

Thou shalt not stir a foot to seek a foe.

*(Enter **prince**, with attendants)*

PRINCE

Rebellious subjects, enemies to peace, profaners of this neighbour-stained steel,--Will they not hear? What, ho! you men, you beasts, that quench the fire of your pernicious rage with purple fountains issuing from your veins, on pain of torture, from those bloody hands throw your mistemper'd weapons to the ground, and hear the sentence of your moved prince. Three civil brawls, bred of an airy word, by thee, old Capulet, and Montague, have thrice disturb'd the quiet of our streets, and made Verona's ancient citizens cast by their grave beseeming ornaments, to wield old partisans, in hands as old, canker'd with peace, to part your canker'd hate: if ever you disturb our streets again, your lives shall pay the forfeit of the peace. For this time, all the rest depart away: you Capulet; shall go along with me: and, Montague, come you this afternoon, to know our further pleasure in this case, to old Free-town, our common judgment-place. Once more, on pain of death, all men depart.

*(Exeunt all but **Montague**, **Lady Montague**, and **Benvolio**)*

MONTAGUE

Who set this ancient quarrel new abroach? Speak, nephew, were you by when it began?

O R I G I N A L   T E X T

LADY MONTAGUE

You're not throwing hands with anyone today fam!

*(**Prince Escalus** makes his entrance with his entourage)*

PRINCE

(Raising his voice to the crowd) Ye heathens! You are totally killing the vibe, brawling with thy brethren? Gassing each other up to the point of carnage! I'll have you all yeeted if you don't sheathe your swords and listen to me! *(**Montagues** and **Capulets**, shook, disarm themselves)* Three times now your drama has ruined the cities peace era, simply because you, Capulet, and you, Montague, cannot just simply leave each other on read. Ever do we require the commoners to sever your brawls. Disturb our vibe again, and I shall cancel thee from this realm! The rest, begone! *(To **Capulet**)* You, Capulet, roll with me. *(To **Montague**)* Montague, slide unto my DMs later, I have more to discourse with thee. All else, dip.

*(Everyone exits except for **Montague**, **Lady Montague**, and **Benvolio**)*

MONTAGUE

Spill the tea, kinsman. Thou were present when it all popped off?

BENVOLIO

Here were the servants of your adversary, and yours, close fighting ere I did approach: I drew to part them: in the instant came the fiery Tybalt, with his sword prepared, which, as he breathed defiance to my ears, he swung about his head and cut the winds, who nothing hurt withal hiss'd him in scorn: while we were interchanging thrusts and blows, came more and more and fought on part and part, till the prince came, who parted either part.

LADY MONTAGUE

O, where is Romeo? saw you him to-day? Right glad I am he was not at this fray.

BENVOLIO

Madam, an hour before the worshipp'd sun peer'd forth the golden window of the east, a troubled mind drave me to walk abroad; where, underneath the grove of sycamore that westward rooteth from the city's side, so early walking did I see your son: towards him I made, but he was ware of me and stole into the covert of the wood: I, measuring his affections by my own, that most are busied when they're most alone, pursued my humour not pursuing his, and gladly shunn'd who gladly fled from me.

BENVOLIO

Facts, the squad was giving the opps some smoke when I arrived. I whipped out my weapon to stop the hostilities, but that's when Tybalt arrived, and started doing the most. That punk was all in my grill and started to throw hands, I was about to secure the dub when the prince rolled up.

LADY MONTAGUE

Hey, where is Romeo? Have you seen him today? I am relieved he didn't catch any of this smoke.

BENVOLIO

Frfr, Lady M. I saw your son Romeo at dawn. The lad seemed to be all up in his feels. I tried to say what up, but it seemed like he was vibing and low-key wanted me-time. So, I just left him to be in his feels.

MONTAGUE

Many a morning hath he there been seen, with tears augmenting the fresh morning dew. Adding to clouds more clouds with his deep sighs; but all so soon as the all-cheering sun should in the furthest east begin to draw the shady curtains from Aurora's bed, away from the light steals home my heavy son, and private in his chamber pens himself, shuts up his windows, locks far daylight out and makes himself an artificial night: black and portentous must this humour prove, unless good counsel may the cause remove.

BENVOLIO

My noble uncle, do you know the cause?

MONTAGUE

I neither know it nor can learn of him.

BENVOLIO

Have you importuned him by any means?

MONTAGUE

Both by myself and many other friends: but he, his own affections' counsellor, is to himself--I will not say how true-- but to himself so secret and so close, so far from sounding and discovery, as is the bud bit with an envious worm, ere he can spread his sweet leaves to the air, or dedicate his beauty to the sun. Could we but learn from whence his sorrows grow. We would as willingly give cure as know.

MONTAGUE

No cap, he has been seen there often, roaming in tears, as if his favorite show got canceled. As the sun rises, he retreats to his room, evading the light. He has barricaded himself, alone in his room, shunning the daylight, just chillin' in his self-made shadow. Indeed, it's an entire vibe.

BENVOLIO

Uncle, do you know why he is all up in his feels?

MONTAGUE

Nay, the lad's lips are sealed, he won't spill any tea.

BENVOLIO

Have you tried to get him to spill?

MONTAGUE

Facts, I have tried, but the kid's a riddle, even to himself I bet. It's like a demon is gnawing at his core. O' that we someday might vibe check his sorrow.

*(Enter **Romeo**)*

BENVOLIO

See, where he comes: so please you, step aside; I'll know his grievance, or be much denied.

MONTAGUE

I would thou wert so happy by thy stay, to hear true shrift. Come, madam, let's away. *(Exeunt **Montague** and **Lady Montague**)*

BENVOLIO

Good-morrow, cousin.

ROMEO

Is the day so young?

BENVOLIO

But new struck nine.

ROMEO

Ay me! sad hours seem long. Was that my father that went hence so fast?

*(Here enters **Romeo**)*

BENVOLIO

Lo, the main character himself. Bounce, would ya? I aim to shoot my shot.

MONTAGUE

I trust you to capture the deets. *(To his wife)* Let's dip.

BENVOLIO

What's good, fam?

ROMEO

Seems quite early still, does it not?

BENVOLIO

Nay, it's like nine.

ROMEO

Bro, the hours creep when joy is absent.

BENVOLIO

It was. What sadness lengthens Romeo's hours?

ROMEO

Not having that, which, having, makes them short.

BENVOLIO

In love?

ROMEO

Out--

BENVOLIO

Of love?

ROMEO

Out of her favour, where I am in love.

BENVOLIO

Alas, that love, so gentle in his view, should be so tyrannous and rough in proof!

BENVOLIO

What burdens thy spirit, fam?

ROMEO

I lack that certain something, the sort that quickens the hour.

BENVOLIO

Oh, so you're catching feelings?

ROMEO

No, 'tis that feelings have caught me, then bounced.

BENVOLIO

Have you fallen from love's grace?

ROMEO

Nay, I hold love for one, yet love leaves me on read.

BENVOLIO

'Tis harsh, brother. But it do be like that sometimes.

ROMEO

Alas, that love, whose view is muffled still, should, without eyes, see pathways to his will! Where shall we dine? O me! What fray was here? yet tell me not, for I have heard it all. Here's much to do with hate, but more with love. Why, then, O brawling love! O loving hate! O any thing, of nothing first create! O heavy lightness! serious vanity! Mis-shapen chaos of well-seeming forms! Feather of lead, bright smoke, cold fire, sick health! Still-waking sleep, that is not what it is! This love feel I, that feel no love in this. Dost thou not laugh?

BENVOLIO

No, coz, I rather weep.

ROMEO

Good heart, at what?

BENVOLIO

At thy good heart's oppression.

ROMEO

Why, such is love's transgression. Griefs of mine own lie heavy in my breast, which thou wilt propagate, to have it prest with more of thine: this love that thou hast shown doth add more grief to too much of mine own. Love is a smoke raised with the fume of sighs; being purged, a fire sparkling in lovers' eyes; being vex'd a sea nourish'd with lovers' tears: what is it else? a madness most discreet, a choking gall and a preserving sweet. Farewell, my coz.

ROMEO

I think it's sus, because love should be chill, yet has me doing the most. So, what you wanna eat? (Sees blood) Good God!... Wait, let me guess. They were hating, and you were loving that they were hating, and they hated that you loved it... Then, y'all threw hands. A very poisonous entanglement of love and hate. If we wake up and choose violence, we shall not pass any vibe checks. Why can't we simply revel in the prime of life with friends gathered along the way? Love is bestowed upon all, and it smacks much harder than hate. Yet, no soul matches my energy... Bro, are you laughing?

BENVOLIO

Nay, fam! Your words have reached my heart. *(Dabs away a tear)*

ROMEO

Bruh, what's with the waterworks?

BENVOLIO

Fam, your words just hit different.

ROMEO

Bet, it's a whole mood when affection binds thee tightly. And now your tears add to my sea of melancholy? Bruh, I am drowning in sentiment, and would you hate to let me surface? Love, I say, is like to an ethereal mist of sweet smoke; when its gone, we crave its return. It's as though love, and hate are one; somewhat pleasing, yet leaves a bitter aftertaste when it's gone. Peace, Im out.

BENVOLIO

Soft! I will go along; An if you leave me so, you do me wrong.

ROMEO

Tut, I have lost myself; I am not here; this is not Romeo, he's some other where.

BENVOLIO

Tell me in sadness, who is that you love.

ROMEO

What, shall I groan and tell thee?

BENVOLIO

Groan! why, no. but sadly tell me who.

ROMEO

Bid a sick man in sadness make his will: ah, word ill urged to one that is so ill! In sadness, cousin, I do love a woman.

BENVOLIO

I aim'd so near, when I supposed you loved.

BENVOLIO

Holup, to bail on me now would be most dirty.

ROMEO

I'm going through it, man. I don't even know myself rn.

BENVOLIO

Frfr, who has your heart speaking in cursive?

ROMEO

Are you pressing me to confess?

BENVOLIO

Facts bro, unburden yourself—who is she?

ROMEO

Will you kick me while I'm down bad? It's not that serious, I just love a woman.

BENVOLIO

Indeed, I see you are submerged in deep feels.

ROMEO

A right good mark-man! And she's fair I love.

BENVOLIO

A right fair mark, fair coz, is soonest hit.

ROMEO

Well, in that hit you miss: she'll not be hit with Cupid's arrow; she hath Dian's wit; and, in strong proof of chastity well arm'd, from love's weak childish bow she lives unharm'd. She will not stay the siege of loving terms, nor bide the encounter of assailing eyes, nor ope her lap to saint-seducing gold: O, she is rich in beauty, only poor, that when she dies with beauty dies her store.

BENVOLIO

Then she hath sworn that she will still live chaste?

ROMEO

She hath, and in that sparing makes huge waste, for beauty starved with her severity cuts beauty off from all posterity. She is too fair, too wise, wisely too fair, to merit bliss by making me despair: she hath forsworn to love, and in that vow do I live dead that live to tell it now.

BENVOLIO

Be ruled by me, forget to think of her.

ROMEO

Facts, the maiden I fancy is a solid ten. No cap.

BENVOLIO

I must say, a hot target is the one everybody's shooting their shot at.

ROMEO

Nay, the maiden's profile is set to private, she swerves thirsty DMs. Her presence is not even proclaimed on the gram. A vision, truly, yet she has vowed to maintain a body count of zero.

BENVOLIO

She intends to keep her virginity locked away forever? New fear unlocked!

ROMEO

That is her intent. She remains an enigma, elusive to the pursuit of love. Absent our union, the lineage ends, and her beauty becomes but a memory. She gatekeeps her own grace, and frfr, I sense a total vibe would exist between us.

BENVOLIO

Bro, mark my words. You should go simp for another.

ROMEO

O, teach me how I should forget to think.

BENVOLIO

By giving liberty unto thine eyes; examine other beauties.

ROMEO

'Tis the way to call hers exquisite, in question more: these happy masks that kiss fair ladies' brows being black put us in mind they hide the fair; he that is strucken blind cannot forget the precious treasure of his eyesight lost: show me a mistress that is passing fair, what doth her beauty serve, but as a note where I may read who pass'd that passing fair? Farewell: thou canst not teach me to forget.

BENVOLIO

I'll pay that doctrine, or else die in debt.

(Exeunt)

ROMEO

Bet, teach me to yeet these consuming thoughts!

BENVOLIO

Look upon the scroll of insta, plenty maidens there await thy favor.

ROMEO

It will backfire, and only serve to raise her higher in my esteem. As maidens masked in makeup and filters don't stir my mind, only does she. Once the eye has savored such a sight, It's not so easily forgotten. Her image lives rent free in my head. Farewell, for thy teachings hold no sway over my heart's course.

BENVOLIO

Bet, I shall teach thee, or I'll take the L trying.

(They dip)

ACT ONE

SCENE TWO

*(Enter **Capulet**, **Paris**, and **Servant**)*

CAPULET

But Montague is bound as well as I, in penalty alike; and 'tis not hard, I think, for men so old as we to keep the peace.

PARIS

Of honourable reckoning are you both; and pity 'tis you lived at odds so long. But now, my lord, what say you to my suit?

CAPULET

But saying o'er what I have said before: my child is yet a stranger in the world; she hath not seen the change of fourteen years, let two more summers wither in their pride, ere we may think her ripe to be a bride.

PARIS

Younger than she are happy mothers made.

ACT ONE

SCENE TWO

*(**Capulet** enters with **Count Paris**, followed by **Peter** a servant)*

CAPULET

(Basically, continuing the tea) But aye, Montague has sworn he would chill, as have I, or we must face the consequences. I am not troubled as we OG's can surely vibe in peace.

PARIS

My lord, y'all goated for that, frfr. 'Tis wild that the beef has endured for so long. What do you say about my request?

CAPULET

Well then, I shall again keep it one hundred. My offspring, she is only a chile. Perchance we chill on the matter of her marriage for two seasons more, ya feel?

PARIS

Yet, truly, shorties less in years than she are bound in matrimony and bring forth little ones most joyous.

CAPULET

And too soon marr'd are those so early made. The earth hath swallow'd all my hopes but she, she is the hopeful lady of my earth: but woo her, gentle Paris, get her heart, my will to her consent is but a part; An she agree, within her scope of choice lies my consent and fair according voice. This night I hold an old accustom'd feast, whereto I have invited many a guest, such as I love; and you, among the store, one more, most welcome, makes my number more. At my poor house look to behold this night Earth-treading stars that make dark heaven light: such comfort as do lusty young men feel when well-apparell'd April on the heel of limping winter treads, even such delight among fresh female buds shall you this night inherit at my house; hear all, all see, and like her most whose merit most shall be: which on more view, of many mine being one may stand in number, though in reckoning none, come, go with me. *(To **Peter**, handing him a paper)* Go, sirrah, trudge about through fair Verona; find those persons out whose names are written there, and to them say, My house and welcome on their pleasure stay.

*(Exeunt **Capulet** and **Paris**)*

PETER

Find them out whose names are written here! It is written, that the shoemaker should meddle with his yard, and the tailor with his last, the fisher with his pencil, and the painter with his nets; but I am sent to find those persons whose names are here writ, and can never find what names the writing person hath here writ. I must to the learned.--In good time.

*(Enter **Benvolio** and **Romeo**)*

CAPULET

Ay, no cap, but such young queens do mature way too fast. Make thy rizz and I shall let thee cook. Try to have her catch feels for you, and if she be inclined to link up. I shall support it with my blessing and good vibes. Listen, I am to host a banger this afternoon. My squad shall join, and I intend to inscribe thy name upon the VIP list. Present yourself at my dwelling tonight, and you can vibe with young queens of plenty, and if that's your ick, survey and select at will, and choose whichever seems a snack to thine eyes. Once you have surveyed the gathering with all these baddies, perhaps my daughter will not seem your paramount choice any longer. Come with me, let's roll. *(To **Peter**, handing him a paper)* Aye, fam, skrrrt across town and summon thy crew, their names be inscribed upon this scroll, let'em know they are squad goals at my house tonight.

*(**Capulet** and **Paris** Exit)*

PETER

Must I search for the peeps inscribed upon this scroll, frfr? They say to embrace new things, and a jack of all trades is better than a master of one. Yet here am I, charged to seek out these peeps, and bruh, I can't even read! I venture alone with no GPS to guide my path. But look, here comes some potential real ones, maybe they can come in clutch.

*(**Benvolio** and **Romeo** arrive)*

BENVOLIO

Tut, man, one fire burns out another's burning, one pain is
lessen'd by another's anguish; turn giddy, and be holp by backward
turning; one desperate grief cures with another's languish: take
thou some new infection to thy eye, and the rank poison of the
old will die.

ROMEO

Your plaintain-leaf is excellent for that.

BENVOLIO

For what, I pray thee?

ROMEO

For your broken shin.

BENVOLIO

Why, Romeo, art thou mad?

ROMEO

Not mad, but bound more than a mad-man is; shut up in prison,
kept without my food, whipp'd and tormented and--God-den,
good fellow.

PETER

God gi' god-den. I pray, sir, can you read?

BENVOLIO

*(To **Romeo**)* Have faith, for you can nerf the burn of heartache by igniting another flame. Cuff a new baddie, and your former anguish will be yoinked to the void.

ROMEO

A plantain leaf slaps for that, too.

BENVOLIO

For heartbreak?

ROMEO

Nay, for when you yeet your shin, Bruh.

BENVOLIO

Say what? Romeo, you wild!

ROMEO

Not wild, but bound more than a madman is, shut up in prison, kept without food, whipped and tormented and- *(Says to **Peter**)* Sup, bro.

PETER

Bless up my guy. Forgive my interruption, but are thou versed in reading?

ROMEO

Ay, mine own fortune in my misery.

PETER

Perhaps you have learned it without book: but, I pray, can you read any thing you see?

ROMEO

Ay, if I know the letters and the language.

PETER

Ye say honestly: rest you merry!

ROMEO

Stay, fellow; I can read. *(Reads)* 'Signior Martino and his wife and daughters; County Anselme and his beauteous sisters; the lady widow of Vitravio; Signior Placentio and his lovely nieces; Mercutio and his brother Valentine; mine uncle Capulet, his wife and daughters; my fair niece Rosaline; Livia; Signior Valentio and his cousin Tybalt, Lucio and the lively Helena.' A fair assembly: whither should they come?

PETER

Up.

ROMEO

Yea, reading between the lines, and seeing this ain't it.

PETER

But frfr, are you capable of reading a script set before you?

ROMEO

Yea, if the script's in a dialect I'm familiar with.

PETER

(Thinking "This fool can't read") A'ight, respect for keepin' it real. I shall take my leave.

ROMEO

Holup, bruh. I got this. *(He checks the invite)* "Yo, Signor Martino and his squad, Count Anselme and the sisters, Vitruvio's bae, Signor Placentio with his nieces, Mercutio and his bro Valentine, Uncle Capulet with his fam, Rosaline and Livia, Signor Valentio and his bro Tybalt, Lucio and that wild one Helena."

Dope lineup. Where they all heading?

PETER

Up.

ROMEO

Whither?

PETER

To supper; to our house.

ROMEO

Whose house?

PETER

My master's.

ROMEO

Indeed, I should have ask'd you that before.

PETER

Now I'll tell you without asking: my master is the great rich Capulet; and if you be not of the house of Montagues, I pray, come and crush a cup of wine. Rest you merry!

(Exit)

ROMEO

Up where? We talking dinner?

PETER

To the crib.

ROMEO

And whose crib is that?

PETER

The Masters.

ROMEO

Bet, I should have asked you that before.

PETER

Now, I'll tell you without you having to ask. My master is the dope and honorable Capulet, and as long you're not a Montague, come smash some wine and chill. Later bros!
*(**Peter** dips)*

BENVOLIO

At this same ancient feast of Capulet's Sups the fair Rosaline whom thou so lovest, with all the admired beauties of Verona: go thither; and, with unattainted eye, compare her face with some that I shall show, and I will make thee think thy swan a crow.

ROMEO

When the devout religion of mine eye maintains such falsehood, then turn tears to fires; and these, who often drown'd could never die, transparent heretics, be burnt for liars! One fairer than my love! the all-seeing sun Ne'er saw her match since first the world begun.

BENVOLIO

Tut, you saw her fair, none else being by, herself poised with herself in either eye: but in that crystal scales let there be weigh'd your lady's love against some other maid that I will show you shining at this feast, and she shall scant show well that now shows best.

ROMEO

I'll go along, no such sight to be shown, but to rejoice in splendor of mine own.

(Exeunt)

BENVOLIO

That baddie, Rosaline, who you Stan for, will grace the Capulet's VIP feast, amongst all the Verona hotties. Go there and weigh her fineness 'gainst the beauty of damsels I shall reveal unto you. The maiden you are simping for shall seem basic when compared to them.

ROMEO

Bruh, should my own eyes betray me like that, I'd sooner burn them out and condemn them for capping. A maiden finer than my chosen love? Yeah right! Not even the sun has glimpsed a baddie this fine since the Earth first commenced its life era.

BENVOLIO

Bro, you hyped her up having seen no others. She is alone in your lineup. Yet observe when your eyes can truly compare her beauty to these tens at the feast, then you will deem her not but mid.

ROMEO

Agreed, I'll accompany you. Not for desire to cast my affection on another, but merely to gaze upon my one true bae.

(They dip)

ACT ONE

SCENE THREE

*(Enter **Lady Capulet** and **nurse**)*

LADY CAPULET

Nurse, where's my daughter? call her forth to me.

NURSE

Now, by my maidenhead, at twelve year old, I bade her come.
What, lamb! what, ladybird! God forbid! Where's this girl? What,
Juliet!

*(Enter **Juliet**)*

JULIET

How now! who calls?

NURSE

Your mother.

JULIET

Madam, I am here. What is your will?

ACT ONE

SCENE THREE

*(Enter **Lady Capulet** and **nurse**)*

LADY CAPULET

Ayo, nurse! Where's my chile? Holler at her.

NURSE

On God and my tweenage purity, I just texted her. Yo, Juliet! Where are thou girl?

*(**Juliet** rolls in)*

JULIET

Sup? Who's calling me?

NURSE

Yo momma.

JULIET

A'ight! Well, here am I. What's up?

LADY CAPULET

This is the matter:--Nurse, give leave awhile, We must talk in secret:--nurse, come back again; I have remember'd me, thou's hear our counsel. Thou know'st my daughter's of a pretty age.

NURSE

Faith, I can tell her age unto an hour.

LADY CAPULET

She's not fourteen.

NURSE

I'll lay fourteen of my teeth,-- and yet, to my teeth be it spoken, I have but four-- she is not fourteen. How long is it now to Lammas-tide?

LADY CAPULET

A fortnight and odd days.

NURSE

Even or odd, of all days in the year, come Lammas-eve at night shall she be fourteen. Susan and she--God rest all Christian souls!-- were of an age: well, Susan is with God; she was too good for me: but, as I said, on Lammas-eve at night shall she be fourteen; that shall she, marry; I remember it well. 'Tis since the earthquake now eleven years; And she was wean'd,--I never shall forget it,-- Of all the days of the year, upon that day: For I had then laid

LADY CAPULET

Nurse, give us some space. We gotta chat in private. Nay, scratch that nurse, remain here. You're basically fam. Do you know how old Juliet is?

NURSE

On God, I do!

LADY CAPULET

This maiden be not even fourteen.

NURSE

I'd wager my chompers on it if I possessed any left—she is not fourteen. How long 'til Lammastide?

LADY CAPULET

Bout' a fortnight and some odd days away, I reckon.

NURSE

A fortnight and some even days, odd days, whatevs, Juliet's turning fourteen on Lammas Eve. Same birthday as Susan, RIP. Man, Susan's gone, but Jule here is about to level up on Lammas Eve. And yo, that night's imprinted in my memory 'cause of that wild earthquake, what, eleven years back? Got her off my teat that same day—no cap, I'd slathered the girls with some bitter wormwood. Was chilling outside, soaking up some rays by the birdhouse while y'all were kickin' it in Mantua. Nay, I do have wormwood to my dug, Sitting in the sun under the dove-house wall; my lord and you were then at Mantua:-- nay, I do bear a brain:--but, as I said, when it did taste the wormwood on the nipple of my dug and felt it bitter, pretty fool, to see it tetchy and fall out with the dug! Shake quoth the dove-house: 'twas no need, I trow, To bid me trudge: And since that time it is eleven years; for then she could stand alone; nay, by the rood, she could have run and waddled all about; for even the day before, she broke her brow: and then my husband--God be with his soul! a' was a merry man--took up the child: 'Yea,' quoth he, 'dost thou fall upon thy face? thou wilt fall backward when thou hast more wit; wilt thou not, Jule?' and, by my holidame, the pretty wretch left crying and said 'Ay.' To see, now, how a jest shall come about! I warrant, an I should live a thousand years, I never should forget it: 'Wilt thou not, Jule?' quoth he; and, pretty fool, it stinted and said 'Ay.'

LADY CAPULET

Enough of this; I pray thee, hold thy peace.

NURSE

Yes, madam: yet I cannot choose but laugh, to think it should leave crying and say 'Ay.' and yet, I warrant, it had upon its brow a bump as big as a young cockerel's stone; a parlous knock; and it cried bitterly: 'Yea,' quoth my husband,'fall'st upon thy face? Thou wilt fall backward when thou comest to age; Wilt thou not, Jule?' it stinted and said 'Ay.'

JULIET

And stint thou too, I pray thee, nurse, say I.

quite the memory. But, as I said, when she tasted the wormwood on my nipple, she found it so bitter she tried throwing hands with my breast, then the Earthquake had us bouncing like we were in a bounce house. Didn't need no oracle to bid me to dip. But that's old news, though. By that time, she could have a run, and waddle about. Frfr, I remember for even the day before she had smacked her forehead. My husband, RIP, took up the chile and was all, "Dost thou fall upon your face? You will fall backward when you hast more wit, Wilt thou not, Jule?" Swear, she cut the waterworks and was like, "Yup." I remember that sent me so hard! If I'm around forever, I'll never forget that. "Right, Jule?" Like magic, her tear ducts went dry, and she was all, "Yup."

LADY CAPULET

Enough of this. That's it, hold your tongue.

NURSE

Yeah, but frfr that was gold, the young maiden ceased her weeping and uttered "Yup." On God, she had this gnarly knot on her forehead. My guy was all, "Fall'st upon thy face? Thou wilt fall backward when thou are of age. Wilt thou not, Jule?" And she just stopped crying and said "yup."

JULIET

Nurse, you literally have no chill, huh?

NURSE

Peace, I have done. God mark thee to his grace! thou wast the
prettiest babe that e'er I nursed: an I might live to see thee
married once, I have my wish.

LADY CAPULET

Marry, that 'marry' is the very theme I came to talk of. Tell me,
daughter Juliet, How stands your disposition to be married?

JULIET

It is an honour that I dream not of.

NURSE

An honour! were not I thine only nurse, I would say thou hadst
suck'd wisdom from thy teat.

LADY CAPULET

Well, think of marriage now; younger than you, here in Verona,
ladies of esteem, are made already mothers: by my count, I was
your mother much upon these years that you are now a maid.
Thus then in brief: the valiant Paris seeks you for his love.

NURSE

A man, young lady! lady, such a man As all the world--why, he's a
man of wax.

NURSE

A'ight, a'ight, I'll chill. May God choose you to receive his grace, for you were the prettiest baby I ever nursed. If I live to see you get cuffed up, all my wishes will have come true.

LADY CAPULET

Facts! That is the very matter I wished to discuss with you, it's cuffing season now so keep it one hundred, how are you vibing with the idea of marriage?

JULIET

Respectfully, it is an honor that I dream not of.

NURSE

"An honor!" This maiden's a paid actor.

LADY CAPULET

Juliet, understand the assignment. Youths of lesser years are already birthing their likenesses. In truth, I had already begun my motherhood era at your age. Thus, I tell you Paris is high-key Stanning for you.

NURSE

Girl, this dude's the real MVP! The CEO of fine!

LADY CAPULET

Verona's summer hath not such a flower.

NURSE

Nay, he's a flower; in faith, a very flower.

LADY CAPULET

What say you? can you love the gentleman? This night you shall behold him at our feast; read o'er the volume of young Paris' face, and find delight writ there with beauty's pen; examine every married lineament, and see how one another lends content and what obscured in this fair volume lies find written in the margent of his eyes. this precious book of love, this unbound lover, to beautify him, only lacks a cover: the fish lives in the sea, and 'tis much pride for fair without the fair within to hide: that book in many's eyes doth share the glory, that in gold clasps locks in the golden story; so shall you share all that he doth possess, by having him, making yourself no less.

NURSE

No less! nay, bigger; women grow by men.

LADY CAPULET

Speak briefly, can you like of Paris' love?

LADY CAPULET

Frfr, Jules, Verona's summers got nothing on his level of hot!

NURSE

Straight up, he's him!

LADY CAPULET

(To Juliet) What say you, dear? Are thou inclined to swipe right on Paris? Behold his rizz at the feast tonight, let him cook and tell me ain't taken with his vibe. Lose yourself in his eyes for he is merely an "I do" away from a life most fair. No cap, as fish to the deep must venture, thou too must not sleep on such a match. You would share all that he possesses, and by cuffing him up, you would lose nothing.

NURSE

Lose nothing? Women grow by men. If you know what I mean.

LADY CAPULET

Juliet don't leave us on read. You ready to secure the bag?

JULIET

I'll look to like, if looking liking move: but no more deep will I endart mine eye than your consent gives strength to make it fly.

*(Enter **Peter**)*

PETER

Madam, the guests are come, supper served up, you called, my young lady asked for, the nurse cursed in the pantry, and every thing in extremity. I must hence to wait; I beseech you, follow straight.

LADY CAPULET

We follow thee.

NURSE

Go, girl, seek happy nights to happy days.

(Exeunt)

JULIET

I'll give him a chance and trust the algorithm, but I'm not about to catch feels unless he passes your vibe check.

*(Enter **Peter**)*

PETER

Madam, the guests are here, supper served up, they have called for you, people are asking for Juliet, and they are taking shots at the nurse in the pantry, it's wiiild. I must go and serve the guests. I beg you, follow me!

LADY CAPULET

We shall follow. Juliet the count is waiting for you.

NURSE:

Go, girl, seek long nights to happy days.

(They roll out)

ACT ONE

SCENE FOUR

*(Enter **Romeo**, **Mercutio**, **Benvolio**, with five or six Maskers, Torch-bearers, and others)*

ROMEO

What, shall this speech be spoke for our excuse? Or shall we on without a apology?

BENVOLIO

The date is out of such prolixity: we'll have no Cupid hoodwink'd with a scarf, bearing a Tartar's painted bow of lath, scaring the ladies like a crow-keeper; nor no without-book prologue, faintly spoke after the prompter, for our entrance: but let them measure us by what they will; we'll measure them a measure, and be gone.

ROMEO

Give me a torch: I am not for this ambling; being but heavy, I will bear the light.

MERCUTIO

Nay, gentle Romeo, we must have you dance.

ACT ONE

SCENE FOUR

*(Enter **Romeo**, **Mercutio**, **Benvolio**, with others)*

ROMEO:

A'ight, so what's our cover for crashing this party? Or shall we roll in without an apology?

BENVOLIO:

Bruh, throwing down epic yarns is so yesteryear. That's doin too much. You really thought we would roll in flexing like some try-hard Cupids, spooking the honeys with fake arrows? Forget a cringy, rehearsed intro. We shall just say "what up council" and leave it to their pleasure to bid us to enter or not.

ROMEO

Hand me the torch, bro. This eve finds me not in the mood for dancing, I'll keep the lighting in check.

MERCUTIO

Romeo my guy, you cant just sit this one out. Ditch your sorrow and let's turn up.

ROMEO

Not I, believe me: you have dancing shoes with nimble soles: I have a soul of lead so stakes me to the ground I cannot move.

MERCUTIO

You are a lover; borrow Cupid's wings, and soar with them above a common bound.

ROMEO

I am too sore enpierced with his shaft to soar with his light feathers, and so bound, I cannot bound a pitch above dull woe: under love's heavy burden do I sink.

MERCUTIO

And, to sink in it, should you burden love; too great oppression for a tender thing.

ROMEO

Is love a tender thing? it is too rough, too rude, too boisterous, and it pricks like thorn.

MERCUTIO

If love be rough with you, be rough with love; prick love for pricking, and you beat love down. Give me a case to put my visage in: a visor for a visor! what care I what curious eye doth quote deformities? Here are the beetle brows shall blush for me.

ROMEO

Nah, fam, that ain't me. You've got kicks to dance in, but my souls are basically made of lead.

MERCUTIO

But you are a loverboy right? Grow some wings like Cupid and rise to the occasion.

ROMEO

Man, its Cupid's arrow that's got me down bad, I'm too wounded to fly and I'm sinking under the heavy weight of a broken heart.

MERCUTIO

Bruh, but if you let yourself sink, 'tis like smacking love in the face! Love is too delicate for that.

ROMEO

Is love delicate, though? Love's savage! It's too rough, to be delicate.

MERCUTIO

If love claps thy cheeks, you just turn around and clap right back! If love is too rough with thee, be rough right back, and maybe you will come out on top! Slide me that mask, a mask for my other mask. Like, who even cares if some Karen sees my mug? Imma let this mask take the heat.*(They put on masks)*

BENVOLIO

Come, knock and enter; and no sooner in, but every man betake him to his legs.

ROMEO

A torch for me: let wantons light of heart tickle the senseless rushes with their heels, for I am proverb'd with a grandsire phrase; i'll be a candle-holder, and look on. The game was ne'er so fair, and I am done.

MERCUTIO

Tut, dun's the mouse, the constable's own word: if thou art dun, we'll draw thee from the mire of this sir-reverence love, wherein thou stick'st up to the ears. Come, we burn daylight, ho!

ROMEO

Nay, that's not so.

MERCUTIO

I mean, sir, in delay we waste our lights in vain, like lamps by day. Take our good meaning, for our judgment sits five times in that ere once in our five wits.

ROMEO

And we mean well in going to this mask; but 'tis no wit to go.

BENVOLIO

Bet, let's roll in and get to it. As soon as we're through those doors, it's time to work it.

ROMEO

I'll hold the light. You lads can get down with your bad self's. But me? Thou can't suffer an L if thou does not step in the ring. I'mma chill with this light and let y'all shine.

MERCUTIO

Stop being so extra. Your anxiety knows no bounds. We shall pull you out of this funk even if you're buried up to your neck. Chop chop, Romeo, daylight's burning, and we gotta roll!

ROMEO

Burning daylight? Fam, it's night.

MERCUTIO

Bruh, I'm saying we're burning our torches with no purpose, just sitting here, like squandering daylight. That's not even a big brain analogy, it's just common-sense, bro.

ROMEO

It may be a big brain move to just bail on this whole plan.

MERCUTIO

Why, may one ask?

ROMEO

I dream'd a dream to-night.

MERCUTIO

And so did I.

ROMEO

Well, what was yours?

MERCUTIO

That dreamers often lie.

ROMEO

In bed asleep, while they do dream things true.

MERCUTIO

O, then, I see Queen Mab hath been with you.

BENVOLIO

Who's Queen Mab?

MERCUTIO

Why's that, bruh?

ROMEO

I dreamt a dream last night.

MERCUTIO

Same, same.

ROMEO

Well, what was yours?

MERCUTIO

That dreamers often lie.

ROMEO

In bed asleep while they dream things that come true.

MERCUTIO

Oh, word? Thou must've been rolling with Queen Mab.

BENVOLIO

Who's Queen Mab?

MERCUTIO

O, then, I see Queen Mab hath been with you. She is the fairies' midwife, and she comes in shape no bigger than an agate-stone on the fore-finger of an alderman, drawn with a team of little atomies Athwart men's noses as they lie asleep; her wagon-spokes made of long spiders' legs, the cover of the wings of grasshoppers, the traces of the smallest spider's web, the collars of the moonshine's watery beams, her whip of cricket's bone, the lash of film, her wagoner a small grey-coated gnat, not so big as a round little worm Prick'd from the lazy finger of a maid; her chariot is an empty hazel-nut made by the joiner squirrel or old grub, time out o' mind the fairies' coachmakers. and in this state she gallops night by night through lovers' brains, and then they dream of love; O'er courtiers' knees, that dream on court'sies straight, O'er lawyers' fingers, who straight dream on fees,O'er ladies ' lips, who straight on kisses dream, which oft the angry Mab with blisters plagues, because their breaths with sweetmeats tainted are: sometime she gallops o'er a courtier's nose, and then dreams he of smelling out a suit; and sometime comes she with a tithe-pig's tail tickling a parson's nose as a' lies asleep, then dreams, he of another benefice: sometime she driveth o'er a soldier's neck, and then dreams he of cutting foreign throats, of breaches, ambuscadoes, Spanish blades, of healths five-fathom deep; and then anon drums in his ear, at which he starts and wakes, and being thus frighted swears a prayer or two and sleeps again. This is that very Mab That plats the manes of horses in the night, and bakes the elflocks in foul sluttish hairs, which once untangled, much misfortune bodes: this is the hag, when maids lie on their backs, that presses them and learns them first to bear, making them women of good carriage: this is she--

ROMEO

Peace, peace, Mercutio, peace! Thou talk'st of nothing.

MERCUTIO

She's the fairies' midwife, no cap. Smaller than the ice on a councilman's pinky. She skrrts in her whip, pulled by ant-sized beasts, cruisin' over dudes' schnozes while they're catching Z's. Her wheels have spiders' legs for spokes. Grasshopper wings for windows. The seat belts are the webs of spiders. Her driver's a lil' bug in a grey suit. Her chariot? Straight-up a hazelnut shell, crafted by either a woodworking squirrel or an OG grubworm. They've been pimping rides for fairies since way back. Every night, she's in that nutty lowrider, drifting through lovers' minds, sparking that love dream static. She drifts over courtier's knees, they start dreaming 'bout taking bows. Rolls over lawyer's digits, and bam, they're dreaming of cashing out. Glides over ladies' puckers, and straight away, they're dreaming 'bout sucking face. Queen Mab, she sometimes throws shade with lip blisters 'cause their breath's too sweet, gets her salty. Now and then, she might tickle a priest's beak with bit of cash, to get him dreaming 'bout a large donation. Sometimes she rides over a soldier's neck, and he dreams of cutting the throats of his opps, of throwing hands, getting ambushed, swinging Spanish steel, and tipping back epic chalices of booze. Then a beat drops in his head, he wakes shook, spits a few prayers, and it's back to the dreamland for him. This is that very Mab that plaits the manes of horses in the night. Mab's that witchy woman giving virgins those R-rated dreams, schooling them on how to hold down a lover and rock a cradle. She's the real MVP.

ROMEO

Chill, Mercutio. You're speaking in cursive again.

MERCUTIO

True, I talk of dreams, which are the children of an idle brain, begot of nothing but vain fantasy, which is as thin of substance as the air and more inconstant than the wind, who wooes even now the frozen bosom of the north, and, being anger'd, puffs away from thence, turning his face to the dew-dropping south.

BENVOLIO

This wind, you talk of, blows us from ourselves; supper is done, and we shall come too late.

ROMEO

I fear, too early: for my mind misgives some consequence yet hanging in the stars shall bitterly begin his fearful date with this night's revels and expire the term of a despised life closed in my breast by some vile forfeit of untimely death. But He, that hath the steerage of my course, direct my sail! On, lusty gentlemen.

BENVOLIO

Strike, drum.

(Exeunt)

MERCUTIO

Facts, I'm riffing about dreams. They are not but nonsense your brain works up to entertain itself while you sleep.

BENVOLIO

That same nonsense you speak of has gotten us off track. Supper's done, and we shall be late to the function.

ROMEO

I worry that we may slide through too early, I am sus something shall go down this night, something that's going to end up getting me cancelled for good if you know what I mean. But let destiny do its thing and direct my sail. Onward lusty gentlemen.

BENVOLIO

Drop that beat!

(And with that, they roll out, exiting stage left)

ACT ONE

SCENE FIVE

*(Enter **servingmen** with napkins)*

PETER

Where's Potpan, that he helps not to take away? He shift a trencher? he scrape a trencher!

FIRST SERVINGMAN

When good manners shall lie all in one or two men's hands and they unwashed too, 'tis a foul thing.

PETER

Away with the joint-stools, remove the court-cupboard, look to the plate. Good thou, save me a piece of marchpane; and, as thou lovest me, let the porter let in Susan Grindstone and Nell. Antony, and Potpan!

SECOND SERVINGMAN

Ay, boy, ready.

ACT ONE

SCENE FIVE

*(**Peter** and other **servingmen** enter with napkins)*

PETER

Where's Potpan? Bro just dipped out? He should be clearing tables or scraping plates.

FIRST SERVINGMAN

When only one or two bros are keeping it one hundred, and they still leave crumbs, 'tis a foul thing.

PETER

Yeet the stools, the sideboards, fetch the plates. You, save me a piece of that marzipan, fam. No lie, if thou loves me, get the porter to let in Susan Grindstone and Nell. Antony and Potpan!

SECOND SERVINGMAN

Yeah bruh, I'm here.

PETER

You are looked for and called for, asked for and sought for, in the great chamber.

FIRST SERVINGMAN

We cannot be here and there too. Cheerly, boys; be brisk awhile, and the longer liver take all.

*(Enter **Capulet**, with **Juliet** and others of his house, meeting the Guests and Maskers)*

CAPULET

Welcome, gentlemen! Ladies that have their toes unplagued with corns will have a bout with you. Ah ha, my mistresses! Which of you all will now deny to dance? She that makes dainty, she, I'll swear, hath corns; am I come near ye now? Welcome, gentlemen! I have seen the day that I have worn a visor and could tell a whispering tale in a fair lady's ear, such as would please: 'tis gone, 'tis gone, 'tis gone: you are welcome, gentlemen! Come, musicians, play. A hall, a hall! Give room! And foot it, girls. *(Music plays, and they dance)* More light, you knaves; and turn the tables up, and quench the fire, the room is grown too hot. Ah, sirrah, this unlook'd-for sport comes well. Nay, sit, nay, sit, good cousin Capulet; for you and I are past our dancing days: how long is't now since last yourself and I were in a mask?

CAPULET'S COUSIN

By'r lady, thirty years.

PETER

They're looking for you in the great chamber.

FIRST SERVINGMAN

Fam, we can't be in two places at once! Cheers, bros. Work quick, winner takes all.

(Capulet strides in with his squad, **Tybalt, Lady Capulet, Juliet***. They bump into* **Romeo, Benvolio, Mercutio***)*

CAPULET

Welcome, my dudes! Only the maidens with corns on their toes are refusing to dance. Aye girls, who's hittin' the dance floor now? If any maiden refuse, I'll bet she's hiding toe beef! Welcome, bros. Back in my day, I'd mask up and spit some game in some maidens' ears too. Those days are long gone now. Y'all are solid, gents. Let's get it! Musicians, drop that beat! *(The beat drops, they turn up,* **Romeo** *chills solo)* Scooch over, make space, make space. Bust a move, ladies! *(To the* **servingmen***)* We need more lighting, you turkeys! Toss the tables aside and clear the floor! Kill the heat, it's mad hot in here... *(To his* **cousin***)* Aye, my dude, this party's a banger! Chillax, chillax, my Capulet cuz. We're past our dancing era, fam. *(****Capulet*** *and his* **Cousin** *take a seat)* Yo, how long's it been since we rocked masks at a banger like this?

CAPULET'S COUSIN

Sheeesshh, like three decades.

CAPULET

What, man! 'tis not so much, 'tis not so much: 'tis since the nuptials of Lucentio, come pentecost as quickly as it will, some five and twenty years; and then we mask'd.

CAPULET'S COUSIN

'Tis more, 'tis more, his son is elder, sir; his son is thirty.

CAPULET

Will you tell me that? His son was but a ward two years ago.

ROMEO

*(To a **servingman**)* What lady is that, which doth enrich the hand of yonder knight?

SERVINGMAN

I know not, sir.

ROMEO

O, she doth teach the torches to burn bright! It seems she hangs upon the cheek of night like a rich jewel in an Ethiope's ear; beauty too rich for use, for earth too dear! So shows a snowy dove trooping with crows, as yonder lady o'er her fellows shows. The measure done, I'll watch her place of stand, and, touching hers, make blessed my rude hand.

CAPULET

Nay, fam, remember Lucentio's wedding? Let the years fly by as they will, it's been only a quarter century since we were rizzing up the ladies in masks.

CAPULET'S COUSIN

Nay, 'tis been longer. Lucentio's son is full on adulting now, he's hit the big 3-0.

CAPULET

For real? You gonna hit me with that? Dude was still a youngling like, a second ago.

ROMEO

*(To a **servingman**)* Aye, who's the baddie that's blessing the hand of that knight over there?

SERVINGMAN

No clue, my guy.

ROMEO

Oh, she teaches the torches to burn bright! It seems she hangs upon the cheek of night like a rich jewel in an Africans ear. She has more beauty than anyone could ever use. She's too fine for this Earth, she stands out like a white dove flying with crows. When this song is over, I'll take her beautiful hand in mine.

Did my heart love till now? forswear it, sight! For I ne'er saw true beauty till this night.

TYBALT

This, by his voice, should be a Montague. Fetch me my rapier, boy. What dares the slave come hither, cover'd with an antic face, to fleer and scorn at our solemnity? Now, by the stock and honour of my kin, to strike him dead, I hold it not a sin.

CAPULET

Why, how now, kinsman! wherefore storm you so?

TYBALT

Uncle, this is a Montague, our foe, a villain that is hither come in spite, to scorn at our solemnity this night.

CAPULET

Young Romeo is it?

TYBALT

'Tis he, that villain Romeo.

CAPULET

Content thee, gentle coz, let him alone; he bears him like a portly gentleman; and, to say truth, Verona brags of him to be a virtuous and well-govern'd youth: I would not for the wealth of all the town

Did my heart ever love before rn? My eyes were capping then, because I never saw such a stunner till now.

TYBALT

By his voice, I can tell he be a Montague! *(To his **Page**)* Yo, fetch me my steel, lil' bro! Can you believe this dude? Crashing our party with his mug hidden, trolling us? By the fam's honor, it wouldn't be out of pocket to drop him right here!

CAPULET

Whoa, what's good Kinsman? What's got you heated?

TYBALT

Uncle, dude's a Montague—our foe, he's here to clown on us, and crash our party!

CAPULET

Young Romeo, is it?

TYBALT

It's him, that snake, Romeo!

CAPULET

Chill, fam! Let the man be! He's rolling like a true gent, and to tell the truth, Verona brags on him to be all class, I ain't about to diss him in my own crib, not for all the money in the world. So chill,

here in my house do him disparagement: therefore be patient, take no note of him: it is my will, the which if thou respect, show a fair presence and put off these frowns, and ill-beseeming semblance for a feast.

TYBALT

It fits, when such a villain is a guest: I'll not endure him.

CAPULET

He shall be endured: what, goodman boy! I say, he shall: go to; am I the master here, or you? go to. You'll not endure him! God shall mend my soul! You'll make a mutiny among my guests! You will set cock-a-hoop! you'll be the man!

TYBALT

Why, uncle, 'tis a shame.

CAPULET

Go to, go to; you are a saucy boy: is't so, indeed? This trick may chance to scathe you, I know what: you must contrary me! marry, 'tis time. Well said, my hearts! You are a princox; go: be quiet, or-- More light, more light! For shame! I'll make you quiet. What, cheerly, my hearts!

let it slide. It is my will. If you respect me, you will chill out and wipe that scowl off. That ain't the look for a party.

TYBALT

It fits when a poser like him sneaks in! I ain't about to let this slide!

CAPULET

You're gonna chill, fam. You're trippin if you think you're not. Am I the master here, or you? You'll not let it slide? God bless my soul, you'll get us all canceled starting drama with the Montagues!

TYBALT

But unc, he is disrespecting us!

CAPULET

A'ight, a'ight, you little punk! That's how it's going to be? Bet, this stupidity is gonna catch up with you. You want to contradict me? I'll school you real quick *(To the **guests**)* Y'all are killing it, let's keep this party going! *(To **Tybalt**)* You little twerp, sit down and shut up, or else—*(To **servingmen**)* more light, more light! *(To **Tybalt**)* You ought to be ashamed of yourself! *(To the **guests**)* Don't kill the vibe, lets party peeps!

(The beat drops once more, and the crowd starts bustin' moves)

TYBALT

Patience perforce with wilful choler meeting makes my flesh
tremble in their different greeting. I will withdraw: but this
intrusion shall now seeming sweet convert to bitter gall.

(Tybalt exits)

ROMEO

(To Juliet) If I profane with my unworthiest hand this holy shrine,
the gentle fine is this: my lips, two blushing pilgrims, ready stand
to smooth that rough touch with a tender kiss.

JULIET

Good pilgrim, you do wrong your hand too much, which
mannerly devotion shows in this; for saints have hands that
pilgrims' hands do touch, and palm to palm is holy palmers' kiss.

ROMEO

Have not saints lips, and holy palmers too?

JULIET

Ay, pilgrim, lips that they must use in prayer.

ROMEO

O, then, dear saint, let lips do what hands do; they pray, grant
thou, lest faith turn to despair.

TYBALT

This mixture of forced patience and anger has me shook. I'll just dip for now. Romeo may think this is funny, but let's see how funny it is when I catch him lackin'.

(Tybalt exits)

ROMEO

(Taking Juliet's hand) If I am too bold by taking thy hand without deserving to, I'm guilty of a lit sin because my lips, like two blushing pilgrims, are ready to make things better with a kiss that smacks.

JULIET

Kind pilgrim, you're doing your hand wrong, because showing such polite devotion is not wrong, since saints have hands that are touched by pilgrims' hands, and hand to hand is like sucking face for a pilgrim.

ROMEO

Don't saints and pilgrims have lips too?

JULIET

Ay, pilgrim, they have lips they gotta pray with.

ROMEO

Oh, dear saint, let our lips do what hands do. They pray; please grant their wish, otherwise my faith might turn to bad vibes.

JULIET

Saints do not move, though grant for prayers' sake.

ROMEO

Then move not, while my prayer's effect I take. Thus from my lips, by yours, my sin is purged.

JULIET

Then have my lips the sin that they have took.

ROMEO

Sin from thy lips? O trespass sweetly urged! Give me my sin again.

(They kiss again)

JULIET

You kiss by the book.

NURSE

Madam, your mother craves a word with you.

(Juliet moves away)

JULIET

Saints don't take action, even if they agree to a prayer.

ROMEO

Then don't move, while I take the benefit of my prayer. *(He kisses her)* With this kiss my sin you have taken.

JULIET

So you're just going to leave this slimy sin on my lips?

ROMEO

You're right! My bad. Give me my sin back.

(They kiss again)

JULIET

You kiss like you know what you're doing.

NURSE

Babygirl, your momma wants to talk to you.

*(**Juliet** scoots away)*

ROMEO

What is her mother?

NURSE

Marry, bachelor, her mother is the lady of the house, and a good lady, and a wise and virtuous I nursed her daughter, that you talk'd withal; I tell you, he that can lay hold of her shall have the chinks.

ROMEO

Is she a Capulet? O dear account! my life is my foe's debt.

BENVOLIO

Away, begone; the sport is at the best.

ROMEO

Ay, so I fear; the more is my unrest.

CAPULET

Nay, gentlemen, prepare not to be gone; We have a trifling foolish banquet towards. Is it e'en so? why, then, I thank you all I thank you, honest gentlemen; good night. More torches here! Come on then, let's to bed. Ah, sirrah, by my fay, it waxes late: I'll to my rest.

*(Exeunt all but **Juliet** and **nurse**)*

ROMEO

Who is her mother?

NURSE

Well, sir, her mother is the lady of the house, and she's a thicc, smart, and virtuous lady. I was the one who breastfed her daughter, whom you were just chatting with. Let me tell you, he who cuffs her up will be a rich man.

ROMEO

(To himself) She's a Capulet? Bruh, that's like premium trouble. My life is in my opps hands now.

BENVOLIO

(To Romeo) Yo, let's bounce. It doesn't get much better than that!

ROMEO

Facts, but I feel like I just signed up for some major drama.

CAPULET

Nay, gentlemen, y'all can't dip so soon. We got dessert on deck. -- *(Listens to a whisper)* For real? Mad respect to y'all. Peace out. Goodnight. Bring the torches, and let's wrap it up. *(To his cousin)* Bro, it's getting late. Time to crash out.

(Everyone but Juliet and nurse heads out)

JULIET

Come hither, nurse. What is yond gentleman?

NURSE

The son and heir of old Tiberio.

JULIET

What's he that now is going out of door?

NURSE

Marry, that, I think, be young Petrucio.

JULIET

What's he that follows there, that would not dance?

NURSE

I know not.

JULIET

Go ask his name: if he be married. my grave is like to be my
wedding bed.

JULIET

Come here, nurse. Who's that dude?

NURSE

He is the son and heir of old Tiberio.

JULIET

Who's that guy dipping out the door?

NURSE

That, I think is young Petruchio.

JULIET

And that dude behind him, the guy who wouldn't dance?

NURSE

IDK.

JULIET

Go ask his name. *(Nurse exits)* If that guy's taken, I'll legit
die before I get married to someone else.

NURSE

His name is Romeo, and a Montague; the only son of your great
enemy.

JULIET

My only love sprung from my only hate! too early seen unknown,
and known too late! Prodigious birth of love it is to me, that I
must love a loathed enemy.

NUSRE

What's this? what's this?

JULIET

A rhyme I learn'd even now of one I danced withal.

(One calls within 'Juliet')

NURSE

Anon, anon! Come, let's away; the strangers all are gone.

(Exeunt)

NURSE

(Coming back) That's Romeo. He's a Montague. Literally the only child of the fam's opps.

JULIET

(To herself) So, the only guy I love is the son of the only dude I hate? I saw him too quick without knowing the deets, and now it's too late! Love's straight up playing me, got me catching feels for the one I'm supposed to beef with!

NURSE

What's that you're mumbling?

JULIET

Oh, just some bars I heard someone spit tonight.

(Someone shouts, "Juliet!")

NURSE

Bet, bet. Let's roll out. Everyone dipped.

(They SKRRRT off)

ACT TWO
PROLOGUE

(Chorus)

Now old desire doth in his death-bed lie, and young affection gapes to be his heir; that fair for which love groan'd for and would die, with tender Juliet match'd, is now not fair. now Romeo is beloved and loves again, alike betwitched by the charm of looks, but to his foe supposed he must complain, and she steal love's sweet bait from fearful hooks: Being held a foe, he may not have access to breathe such vows as lovers use to swear; and she as much in love, her means much less to meet her new-beloved any where: but passion lends them power, time means, to meet tempering extremities with extreme sweet.

*(The **Chorus** exits)*

ACT TWO
PROLOGUE

(Chorus)

Romeo's old crush is just a memory, a ghost. Now he's thirsty for Juliet and doing the most. He was all about Rosaline, filled with love and lust, but next to Juliet, Rosalines looking dust. The feelings are mutual between Romeo & Juliet. They swiped right on each other and said "Bet". He gives her speeches of love, like a really chill bro. Even though she is supposed to be his foe. And in her eyes, he should inspire dread, an enemy, whose words should be left on read. Romeo just wants to proclaim his love to her, but he can't because of this beef between boomers. And Juliet's so down, but she's got even less play. With how much she loves him she can't even say. But love sparks the vibe, and power it instills, for when time slides them chances for secret thrills. Their love is exploding, and their passion spills, turning danger to delight, giving ultimate chills.

*(The **Chorus** exits)*

ACT TWO

SCENE ONE

*(Enter **Romeo**)*

ROMEO

Can I go forward when my heart is here? Turn back, dull earth, and find thy centre out. He climbs the wall, and leaps down within it.

*(Enter **Benvolio** and **Mercutio**)*

BENVOLIO

Romeo! my cousin Romeo!

MERCUTIO

He is wise; and, on my lie, hath stol'n him home to bed.

BENVOLIO

He ran this way, and leap'd this orchard wall: call, good Mercutio.

ACT TWO

SCENE ONE

*(**Romeo** enters alone)*

ROMEO

Can I peace out when my heart's on lockdown here? Gotta go back to where my heart resides.

*(**Romeo** moves off. **Benvolio** and **Mercutio** enter)*

BENVOLIO

Yo, Romeo! Where you at, fam?

MERCUTIO

Bro's smart. Bet he dipped off to go crash in his bed.

BENVOLIO

He sprinted this way and yeeted himself over the wall. Holler, Mercutio, holler.

MERCUTIO

Nay, I'll conjure too. Romeo! humours! madman! passion! lover! Appear thou in the likeness of a sigh: speak but one rhyme, and I am satisfied; cry but 'Ay me!' pronounce but 'love' and 'dove;' speak to my gossip Venus one fair word, one nick-name for her purblind son and heir, Young Adam Cupid, he that shot so trim, when King Cophetua loved the beggar-maid! He heareth not, he stirreth not, he moveth not; The ape is dead, and I must conjure him. I conjure thee by Rosaline's bright eyes, By her high forehead and her scarlet lip, by her fine foot, straight leg and quivering thigh and the demesnes that there adjacent lie, that in thy likeness thou appear to us!

BENVOLIO

And if he hear thee, thou wilt anger him.

MERCUTIO

This cannot anger him: 'twould anger him to raise a spirit in his mistress' circle of some strange nature, letting it there stand till she had laid it and conjured it down; that were some spite: my invocation is fair and honest, and in his mistres s' name I conjure only but to raise up him.

BENVOLIO

Come, he hath hid himself among these trees, to be consorted with the humorous night: blind is his love and best befits the dark.

MERCUTIO

Bet, I'll raise him up. Romeo! Oh, emo bro! Lover boy! Pop up like a notif. Spit just one bar, and I'm all set. Just drop an "Ah me!" or slide in with "love" and "dove." Toss one sweet word to our girl Venus. Give a shout to her blind son, Cupid, the OG archer of the classic tales. Romeo's ghosting us, won't budge, won't slide. This dude's offline, but I must make him appear. I'm calling you out by Rosaline's fire eyes, by her big ol' forehead and those juicy lips. By her grippers, and her long legs. By her bussin' thighs, curvy hips and other parts! Come on out, in your true form, no disguise!

BENVOLIO

Chill, bro, or you'll get him heated!

MERCUTIO

Nah, no cap, that won't tilt him. He'd rage if I summoned some random spirit for her to get down with, that's what would get him heated! I'm just saying the name of his crush to slide him out of the shadows.

BENVOLIO

Look, bro's gone stealth mode among these trees, to sync up with the moody vibes of the night. His love's blind and loves dark vibes.

MERCUTIO

If love be blind, love cannot hit the mark. Now will he sit under a medlar tree, and wish his mistress were that kind of fruit as maids call medlars, when they laugh alone. Romeo, that she were, O, that she were an open et caetera, thou a poperin pear! Romeo, good night: I'll to my truckle-bed; this field-bed is too cold for me to sleep: come, shall we go?

BENVOLIO

Go, then; for 'tis in vain to seek him here that means not to be found.

(Exeunt)

MERCUTIO

If love's blind, it's missing all the shots. Now he'll be chilling under a medlar tree, wishing his girl was easy pickings, you see. Romeo, if only she was down, oh if only, an open invite, and you'd be less lonely! A'ight, peace out, I'm off to crash at my pad. Sleeping outside is a no-go. We dipping?

BENVOLIO

Let's jet, fam. No use in scouting for a guy who's not trying to be found.

*(**Benvolio** and **Mercutio** exit)*

ACT TWO

SCENE TWO

*(Enter **Romeo**)*

ROMEO

He jests at scars that never felt a wound. (***Juliet*** *appears above at a window)* But, soft! what light through yonder window breaks? It is the east, and Juliet is the sun. Arise, fair sun, and kill the envious moon, who is already sick and pale with grief, that thou her maid art far more fair than she: be not her maid, since she is envious; her vestal livery is but sick and green and none but fools do wear it; cast it off. It is my lady, O, it is my love! O, that she knew she were! She speaks yet she says nothing: what of that? Her eye discourses; I will answer it. I am too bold, 'tis not to me she speaks: Two of the fairest stars in all the heaven, having some business, do entreat her eyes to twinkle in their spheres till they return. What if her eyes were there, they in her head? The brightness of her cheek would shame those stars, as daylight doth a lamp; her eyes in heaven would through the airy region stream so bright that birds would sing and think it were not night. See, how she leans her cheek upon her hand! O, that I were a glove upon that hand, that I might touch that cheek!

JULIET

Ay me!

ACT TWO

SCENE TWO

*(Enter **Romeo**)*

ROMEO

It's easy to roast one's scars, when you yourself have never been scratched. (***Juliet*** *vibes on the balcony*) But, pause! What's glowing through that window? It's the east, and Juliet is the sun. Get up, bussin' sun, and ghost the salty moon, who's already jelly and looks dead tired, because you, my bae, are way more lit than she. Don't be like her bae, she's all salty. Her V-card makes her look sick and green. Only fools hold onto it, so toss it. Oh snap, no cap, it's actually my bae! If only she knew how deep my feels are! She speaks but spills no tea, what's with that? Her eyes speak, I'll DM them back. I'm shooting my shot, no 'tis not to me she speaks. Two of the most lit stars in the whole sky had to go on some quest, they begged her eyes to flex in their spots till they're back. The glow of her cheek claps back at those stars, like the sun outshines a candle. Her eyes in the night sky would make the birds think it's morning. Look, she's resting her cheek in her palm! Oh, if I were the glove on that hand, so, I could touch that cheek!

JULIET

Big mood.

ROMEO

She speaks: O, speak again, bright angel! for thou art as glorious
to this night, being o'er my head as is a winged messenger of
heaven unto the white-upturned wondering eyes of mortals that
fall back to gaze on him when he bestrides the lazy-pacing clouds
and sails upon the bosom of the air.

JULIET

O Romeo, Romeo! wherefore art thou Romeo? Deny thy father
and refuse thy name; or, if thou wilt not, be but sworn my love,
and I'll no longer be a Capulet.

ROMEO

(Aside) Shall I hear more, or shall I speak at this?

JULIET

'Tis but thy name that is my enemy; thou art thyself, though not a
Montague. What's Montague? it is nor hand, nor foot, nor arm,
nor face, nor any other part belonging to a man. O, be some other
name! What's in a name? that which we call a rose by any other
name would smell as sweet; So Romeo would, were he not
Romeo call'd, retain that dear perfection which he owes without
that title. Romeo, doff thy name, and for that name which is no
part of thee take all myself.

ROMEO

I take thee at thy word: Call me but love, and I'll be new baptized;
henceforth I never will be Romeo.

ROMEO

And there she goes: flex those sonnets, radiant angel! You glow
fierce tonight! You're straight fire! Like a legit messenger of the
heavens, mere mortals fall all over themselves just to scope you
sailing on the wind.

JULIET

(Not knowing **Romeo** *hears her)* Like, Romeo, why you gotta be
Romeo? Cancel your dad and switch up your handle. Or if you're
not down, Just say you're into me and I'll ghost the Capulet name.

ROMEO

(To himself) Should I slide into the convo, or let her spill?

JULIET

Your name's the enemy; you're you, even if you weren't a
Montague. What's a Montague? It's neither hand, nor foot, nor
arm, nor face, nor any other part belonging to a bro. So, what if
you had a different tag? What's in a name? That which we call a
rose by any other word would smell just as dope; So would
Romeo, even if he was not a Montague, Romeo would be just as
lit without the Montague title. Romeo, trash your name, and for
that name, which isn't even a part of you, take all of me.

ROMEO

(To **Juliet***)* Bet, I trust your word. Just dub me your main
squeeze, and I'll cop a new @. From now on I'm not Romeo.

JULIET

What man art thou that thus bescreen'd in night so stumblest on my counsel?

ROMEO

By a name I know not how to tell thee who I am: my name, dear saint, is hateful to myself, because it is an enemy to thee; had I it written, I would tear the word.

JULIET

My ears have not yet drunk a hundred words of that tongue's utterance, yet I know the sound: art thou not Romeo and a Montague?

ROMEO

Neither, fair saint, if either thee dislike.

JULIET

How camest thou hither, tell me, and wherefore? The orchard walls are high and hard to climb, and the place death, considering who thou art, if any of my kinsmen find thee here.

ROMEO

With love's light wings did I o'er-perch these walls; for stony limits cannot hold love out, and what love can do that dares love attempt; therefore thy kinsmen are no let to me.

JULIET

Who even are you? Why are you lurking in the shadows eavesdropping on me?

ROMEO

Forget the name, it's just a tag, I can't even vibe with who I am. My label's like a thorn to me, cause it's beef to you! I would delete it if I could!

JULIET

You haven't spit even a hundred words, but your voice's got that blue checkmark. I know it Romeo!

ROMEO

I'll be whatever makes you swipe right!

JULIET

Spill, how'd you get here, and why? The orchard's got walls for days, and this place could be a death trap if my fam caught you creeping.

ROMEO

Cupid gave me wings, and these walls? Low-key basic. What a guy will do for love, he'll yeet over a hundred walls. Any obstacle is like zero probs.

JULIET

If they do see thee, they will murder thee.

ROMEO

Alack, there lies more peril in thine eye than twenty of their swords: look thou but sweet, and I am proof against their enmity.

JULIET

I would not for the world they saw thee here.

ROMEO

I have night's cloak to hide me from their sight; and but thou love me, let them find me here: my life were better ended by their hate, than death prorogued, wanting of thy love.

JULIET

By whose direction found'st thou out this place?

ROMEO

By love, who first did prompt me to inquire; he lent me counsel and I lent him eyes. I am no pilot; yet, wert thou as far as that vast shore wash'd with the farthest sea, I would adventure for such merchandise.

JULIET

But if they see you, you will get murked!

ROMEO

Facts, but one salty look from you hits harder than a squad of
your kin with swords. Just throw me one good vibe, and I'm
chillin', untouchable.

JULIET

I'd give anything just to keep them from clocking you!

ROMEO

The dark's got me cloaked, and if you're not down, then let them
find me. Better to catch that L than to thirst without your love!

JULIET

Who spilled the tea on where my room is?

ROMEO

Love gave me the tea! I ain't no captain, but if you were oceans
away, I'd still pull up for a treasure like you!

JULIET

Thou know'st the mask of night is on my face, else would a
maiden blush bepaint my cheek for that which thou hast heard
me speak to-night fain would I dwell on form, fain, fain deny what
I have spoke: but farewell compliment! Dost thou love me? I
know thou wilt say 'Ay,' And I will take thy word: yet if thou
swear'st, thou mayst prove false; at lovers' perjuries then say, Jove
laughs. O gentle Romeo, If thou dost love, pronounce it faithfully:
or if thou think'st I am too quickly won, I'll frown and be perverse
an say thee nay so thou wilt woo; but else, not for the world. In
truth, fair Montague, I am too fond, and therefore thou mayst
think my 'havior light: but trust me, gentleman, I'll prove more
true than those that have more cunning to be strange. I should
have been more strange, I must confess, but that thou
overheard'st, ere I was ware, my true love's passion: therefore
pardon me, and not impute this yielding to light love, which the
dark night hath so discovered.

ROMEO

Lady, by yonder blessed moon I swear that tips with silver all
these fruit-tree tops--

JULIET

O, swear not by the moon, the inconstant moon, that monthly
changes in her circled orb, lest that thy love prove likewise
variable.

ROMEO

What shall I swear by?

JULIET

The night's hiding my face, otherwise, you'd see me blushing hard from what you overheard tonight. I could front and play it off all cool, but real talk: are we a thing? I feel you'll say "yeah," and I'm down for that, but if you're just playing me... They say, love's a game, and Jove's lol'ing at us. But Romeo, my dude, if you're about this life, say it like you mean it. Or if you think I'm easy, I'll play hard to get, and make you work for it, unless you're not serious. Frfr, I'm feeling you too much, which might make me seem basic, but I'm legit, and I'll show you I'm not just playing. I should've played it more mysterious I guess, but you caught my love confession by accident. So forgive me, and don't think I'm just about that fling life, because the night just showed you what's up.

ROMEO

Aight, I swear on the moon up there, the one that shines like a filter on the fruit trees.

JULIET

Nah, don't put that on the moon. That dude changes up every single month. I need us to be more solid than that, no cap.

ROMEO

So, what should I put it on?

JULIET

Do not swear at all; or, if thou wilt, swear by thy gracious self, which is the god of my idolatry, and I'll believe thee.

ROMEO

If my heart's dear love--

JULIET

Well, do not swear: although I joy in thee, I have no joy of this contract to-night: It is too rash, too unadvised, too sudden; too like the lightning, which doth cease to be ere one can say 'It lightens.' Sweet, good night! this bud of love, by summer's ripening breath, may prove a beauteous flower when next we meet. Good night, good night! as sweet repose and rest come to thy heart as that within my breast!

ROMEO

O, wilt thou leave me so unsatisfied?

JULIET

What satisfaction canst thou have to-night?

ROMEO

The exchange of thy love's faithful vow for mine.

JULIET

Don't swear, like, at all. Or if you're hyped to swear, pinky promise on your life, that you will always be the main character of my heart, and I'll be like, "I trust you, fam."

ROMEO

Cross my heart—

JULIET

Hold up, drop the swears. You're giving me all the feels, but this promise swap is hella rushed. It's like a viral trend: here one second, gone the next. Let's just vibe and see if this blooms. Goodnight, boo. Let's hope this feels as sweet tomorrow.

ROMEO

You gonna leave me on read like that?

JULIET

What kind of DMs were you hoping for tonight?

ROMEO

Slide me a promise of real love, and it's all good.

JULIET

I gave thee mine before thou didst request it: and yet I would it
were to give again.

ROMEO

Wouldst thou withdraw it? for what purpose, love?

JULIET

But to be frank, and give it thee again. And yet I wish but for the
thing I have: my bounty is as boundless as the sea, my love as
deep; the more I give to thee, the more I have, for both are
infinite. *(**Nurse** calls within)* I hear some noise within; dear love,
adieu! Anon, good nurse! Sweet Montague, be true. Stay but a
little, I will come again.

(Exit, above)

ROMEO

O blessed, blessed night! I am afeard. Being in night, all this is but
a dream, too flattering-sweet to be substantial.

*(Re-enter **Juliet**, above)*

JULIET

Three words, dear Romeo, and good night indeed. If that thy bent
of love be honourable, thy purpose marriage, send me word to-

JULIET

Fam, I already hit you with an "I love you" before you even asked.
I wish I could unsend it just to drop it on you one more time!

ROMEO

You'd unsend? But why would you play me like that?

JULIET

Just so I could double-tap that love and hit you up with it again!
But real talk, I'm already all in. My love's deep; the more I vibe
with you, the deeper it gets, 'cause love's like that, endless.

*(Offstage, **nurse** is like, "Juliet, where you at?")*

What's this noise? BRB, just gotta check on the fam. Stick
around, my Montague. Don't ghost me. I'll be right back.

*(**Juliet** exits)*

ROMEO

Man, this night is straight fire! I'm so shook. Feels like I'm just
dreaming this whole situation.

*(**Juliet** pops back on her balcony)*

JULIET

Yo, just a few words Romeo, then it's "night, night" for real. If
you're down for the long haul and not just playing me, hit me up

morrow, by one that I'll procure to come to thee, where and what time thou wilt perform the rite; and all my fortunes at thy foot I'll lay and follow thee my lord throughout the world.

NURSE

(Within) Madam!

JULIET

I come, anon.--But if thou mean'st not well, I do beseech thee—

NURSE

(Within) Madam!

JULIET

By and by, I come:-- to cease thy suit, and leave me to my grief: to-morrow will I send.

ROMEO

So thrive my soul--

JULIET

A thousand times good night!

(Exit, above)

tomorrow. I'll send my squad to scope out the deets, and we'll set a time for us to say our "I do's". I'll throw down my fortunes at your feet, and roll with you wherever, you're my world now!

NURSE

(Yelling from another room) Yo, Juliet!

JULIET

*(To **nurse**)* Bet, hold up! *(To **Romeo**)* But if you're playing me, I can't even.

NURSE

(Still yelling) Juliet!

JULIET

I said I'm coming! Chill! *(To **Romeo**)* Look, if you're just sliding into my DMs, I beg you-

ROMEO

You're my lock screen and home screen.

JULIET

Goodnight a thousand times.

*(**Juliet** dips out)*

ROMEO

A thousand times the worse, to want thy light. love goes toward love, as schoolboys from their books, but love from love, toward school with heavy looks. *(Retiring)*

*(Re-enter **Juliet**, above)*

JULIET

Hist! Romeo, hist! O, for a falconer's voice, to lure this tassel-gentle back again! bondage is hoarse, and may not speak aloud; else would I tear the cave where Echo lies, and make her airy tongue more hoarse than mine, with repetition of my Romeo's name.

ROMEO

It is my soul that calls upon my name: how silver-sweet sound lovers' tongues by night, like softest music to attending ears!

JULIET

Romeo!

ROMEO

My dear?

JULIET

At what o'clock to-morrow shall I send to thee?

ROMEO

Feels a thousand times worse without you. When you're with your bae, you feel like a kid ditching school, but when your bae leaves it's as miserable as walking to school Monday morning.

*(**Romeo** is about to leave, but **Juliet** is back on her balcony)*

JULIET

Yo, Romeo, wait! Wish I could whistle loud like a falconer, to get my boo back here in a flash! Gotta keep it down, or else I'd wake up the whole house with an echo of "My Romeo!" on repeat.

ROMEO

My boo has my name in her voice. Hearing our names in each other's voices slaps, no playlist compares.

JULIET

Romeo!

ROMEO

What's good my little falcon?

JULIET

What time should I slide into your DMs tomorrow?

ROMEO

At the hour of nine.

JULIET

I will not fail: 'tis twenty years till then. I have forgot why I did call thee back.

ROMEO

Let me stand here till thou remember it.

JULIET

I shall forget, to have thee still stand there, remembering how I love thy company.

ROMEO

And I'll still stay, to have thee still forget, forgetting any other home but this.

JULIET

'Tis almost morning; I would have thee gone: and yet no further than a wanton's bird; who lets it hop a little from her hand, like a poor prisoner in his twisted gyves, and with a silk thread plucks it back again so loving-jealous of his liberty.

ROMEO

I would I were thy bird.

ROMEO

Hit me up at nine.

JULIET

I won't ghost. This wait will feel like decades. I forgot why I
even called you back.

ROMEO

I'll chill here until you remember.

JULIET

I'll probably keep forgetting, and you'll be stuck standing there.
But lowkey, I just don't want to close this chat.

ROMEO

I'll stay logged in here, till I get kicked.

JULIET

It's nearly daylight. I wanna say "peace out," but I'm like that kid
who lets his pet bird fly but then yanks it back 'cause he can't let
go.

ROMEO

I'm just saying, it'd be lit if I were your bird.

JULIET

Sweet, so would I: yet I should kill thee with much cherishing.

Good night, good night! parting is such sweet sorrow, that I shall say good night till it be morrow.

(Exit above)

ROMEO

Sleep dwell upon thine eyes, peace in thy breast! Would I were sleep and peace, so sweet to rest! hence will I to my ghostly father's cell, his help to crave, and my dear hap to tell.

(Exit)

JULIET

Facts, but I'd end up giving you too many cuddles. Catch some
Z's, fam. It's mad bittersweet to say goodnight.

(Juliet bounces out)

ROMEO

Sleep tight. If only I could be Mr. Sandman, just to chill with you
all night. Time to slide into my priest's DMs for some real talk
and spill about this dope match.

(He dips out)

ACT TWO

SCENE THREE

*(Enter **Friar Laurence**, with a basket)*

FRIAR LAURENCE

The grey-eyed morn smiles on the frowning night, chequering the eastern clouds with streaks of light, and flecked darkness like a drunkard reels from forth day's path and Titan's fiery wheels: now, ere the sun advance his burning eye, the day to cheer and night's dank dew to dry, I must up-fill this osier cage of ours with baleful weeds and precious-juiced flowers. The earth that's nature's mother is her tomb; what is her burying grave that is her womb, and from her womb children of divers kind we sucking on her natural bosom find, many for many virtues excellent, none but for some and yet all different. O, mickle is the powerful grace that lies in herbs, plants, stones, and their true qualities: for nought so vile that on the earth doth live but to the earth some special good doth give, nor aught so good but strain'd from that fair use revolts from true birth, stumbling on abuse: virtue itself turns vice, being misapplied; and vice sometimes by action dignified. Within the infant rind of this small flower poison hath residence and medicine power: for this, being smelt, with that part cheers each part; being tasted, slays all senses with the heart. Two such opposed kings encamp them still In man as well as herbs, grace and rude will; and where the worser is predominant, full soon the canker death eats up that plant.

ACT TWO

SCENE THREE

*(**Friar Laurence** enters by himself, carrying a basket)*

FRIAR LAURENCE

Yo, the morning's smiling, kicking night's gloom to the curb. Checkin' the sky's vibe making sure it's lit. Now, I gotta stuff this basket with some weeds and medical flowers. The Earth's the mother of nature but also nature's grave. Plants glow up from the dirt, then they peace out in it when their time's up. Out of Earth's belly, a whole squad of plants and critters roll out, and Earth's low-key like a five-star chef to her earthlings, dishing out meals that slap. Every creation's got its own flex, no cap. Herbs, plants, rocks—they all got mad skills. Nothing's so whack on Earth that it can't drop something special. And nothing's so lit that it can't go beast mode if you twist it. Straight-up goodness can flip to badness if you play it wrong. And sometimes, badness flips to chillness with the right vibes. Inside this tiny bud, it's packing both poison and the cure. Sniff it, and you're feeling lit for days. Taste it, and it's game over. Everything's got this yin and yang, In dudes as well as in plants—chill and sus vibes. When the sus vibes take over, it's a quick fade to black.

*(Enter **Romeo**)*

ROMEO

Good morrow, father.

FRIAR LAURENCE

Benedicite! What early tongue so sweet saluteth me? Young son,
it argues a distemper'd head so soon to bid good morrow to thy
bed: care keeps his watch in every old man's eye, and where care
lodges, sleep will never lie; but where unbruised youth with
unstuff'd brain doth couch his limbs, there golden sleep doth
reign: therefore thy earliness doth me assure thou art up-roused
by some distemperature; or if not so, then here I hit it right, our
Romeo hath not been in bed to-night.

ROMEO

That last is true; the sweeter rest was mine.

FRIAR LAURENCE

God pardon sin! wast thou with Rosaline?

ROMEO

With Rosaline, my ghostly father? no; I have forgot that name,
and that name's woe.

*(**Romeo** enters)*

ROMEO

Sup, pops.

FRIAR LAURENCE

Blessings! Who's this hitting me up this early? Bruh, it's sus you're
out of bed at this hour. Old heads are up with the worries, tossing
and turning, but you young guns should be zonked out with zero
worries. You should've been clocking some serious Zs. So, if
you're not tripping over something, it's gotta be because you didn't
hit the sheets at all last night, did you, Romeo?

ROMEO

You got it, F.L. I caught better vibes than sleep could ever give.

FRIAR LAURENCE

Hope you didn't catch any sin along with those vibes! You weren't
with Rosaline, were you?

ROMEO

Rosaline? Nah, she's old news.

FRIAR LAURENCE

That's my good son: but where hast thou been, then?

ROMEO

I'll tell thee, ere thou ask it me again. I have been feasting with mine enemy, where on a sudden one hath wounded me, that's by me wounded: both our remedies within thy help and holy physic lies: I bear no hatred, blessed man, for, lo, my intercession likewise steads my foe.

FRIAR LAURENCE

Be plain, good son, and homely in thy drift; riddling confession finds but riddling shrift.

ROMEO

Then plainly know my heart's dear love is set on the fair daughter of rich Capulet: as mine on hers, so hers is set on mine; and all combined, save what thou must combine by holy marriage: when and where and how we met, we woo'd and made exchange of vow, I'll tell thee as we pass; but this I pray, that thou consent to marry us to-day.

FRIAR LAURENCE

Holy Saint Francis, what a change is here! Is Rosaline, whom thou didst love so dear, so soon forsaken? Young men's love then lies not truly in their hearts, but in their eyes. Jesu Maria, what a deal of brine hath wash'd thy sallow cheeks for Rosaline! How much salt water thrown away in waste, to season love, that of it doth not taste! The sun not yet thy sighs from heaven clears, thy old groans

FRIAR LAURENCE

Right on, my dude. So, where you been tonight?

ROMEO

I'll spill before you even ask, F.L. I've been chilling with the opposition. Outta nowhere, got hit by Cupid's arrow and it was like, KO. You got that holy touch to make us official. You'll do it, right? 'Cause this favor's a win-win for both sides. Frfr.

FRIAR LAURENCE

Keep it a hundred fam, cut through the noise; you are speaking in cursive.

ROMEO

Here's the scoop: I'm all about Juliet—the Capulet it girl. She's feeling me, and I'm feeling her. So, we need you to lock it in with the "I do's". I'll fill you in on the deets later. But for now, I'm down on bended knee: hook us up with a wedding today, yeah?

FRIAR LAURENCE

Whoa, Saint Francis, talk about a plot twist! Ditched Rosaline that fast, huh? Guess guys really do shop with their eyes, not with their hearts. Man, you shed enough tears for Rosaline to flood the city. You've still got the old sob story written all over your face. If you ever were truly into Rosaline, and those feels were legit... and now

ring yet in my ancient ears; lo, here upon thy cheek the stain doth sit of an old tear that is not wash'd off yet: if e'er thou wast thyself and these woes thine, thou and these woes were all for Rosaline: and art thou changed? pronounce this sentence then, women may fall, when there's no strength in men.

ROMEO

Thou chid'st me oft for loving Rosaline.

FRIAR LAURENCE

For doting, not for loving, pupil mine.

ROMEO

And bad'st me bury love.

FRIAR LAURENCE

Not in a grave, to lay one in, another out to have.

ROMEO

I pray thee, chide not; she whom I love now doth grace for grace and love for love allow; the other did not so.

you've flipped the script? Let's get real then: don't expect your girl to stay if you're playing musical chairs with your heart.

ROMEO

You always roasted me over Rosaline.

FRIAR LAURENCE

I never roasted you, my dude. I was trying to wake you up from that obsession, not the love part.

ROMEO

And you were like, "stop Stanning."

FRIAR LAURENCE

Not "stop Stanning", just Stan for another, bruh.

ROMEO

Come on, don't punish me! Juliet's the real deal, and she is mad into me. Rosaline? Not so much.

FRIAR LAURENCE

O, she knew well thy love did read by rote and could not spell.
But come, young waverer, come, go with me, in one respect I'll
thy assistant be; for this alliance may so happy prove, to turn your
households' rancour to pure love.

ROMEO

O, let us hence; I stand on sudden haste.

FRIAR LAURENCE

Wisely and slow; they stumble that run fast.

(Exeunt)

FRIAR LAURENCE

You think you got rizz, but you're a paid actor. A'ight, young flip-flopper, roll with me, i'll back you up on this one thing; this might just be the clutch play to turn your fams' beef into an epic love story.

ROMEO

Bet, we gotta book it, like, yesterday.

FRIAR LAURENCE

Get off the gas, bruh. Slow and steady's the way. Haste makes waste, fam.

(And off they roll)

ACT TWO

SCENE FOUR

*(Enter **Benvolio** and **Mercutio**)*

MERCUTIO

Where the devil should this Romeo be? Came he not home to-night?

BENVOLIO

Not to his father's; I spoke with his man.

MERCUTIO

Ah, that same pale hard-hearted wench, that Rosaline. Torments him so, that he will sure run mad.

BENVOLIO

Tybalt, the kinsman of old Capulet, hath sent a letter to his father's house.

MERCUTIO

A challenge, on my life.

ACT TWO

SCENE FOUR

*(**Benvolio** and **Mercutio** slide onto the scene)*

MERCUTIO

Where's Romeo at, though? Didn't he go home last night?

BENVOLIO

Nah, skipped his dad's crib. I asked a servant.

MERCUTIO

Oof, that ice queen, Rosaline, got him all twisted. Bro's whipped, big time. Dudes delulu!

BENVOLIO

Tybalt, the Capulet's beast, shot a DM to Romeo's spot.

MERCUTIO

I bet he's calling him out.

BENVOLIO

Romeo will answer it.

MERCUTIO

Any man that can write may answer a letter.

BENVOLIO

Nay, he will answer the letter's master, how he dares, being dared.

MERCUTIO

Alas poor Romeo! he is already dead; stabbed with a white wench's black eye; shot through the ear with a love-song; the very pin of his heart cleft with the blind bow-boy's butt-shaft: and is he a man to encounter Tybalt?

BENVOLIO

Why, what is Tybalt?

MERCUTIO

More than prince of cats, I can tell you. O, he is the courageous captain of compliments. He fights as you sing prick-song, keeps time, distance, and proportion; rests me his minim rest, one, two, and the third in your bosom: the very butcher of a silk button, a duellist, a duellist; a gentleman of the very first house, of the first and second cause: ah, the immortal passado! the punto reverso! The hai!

BENVOLIO

Bet Romeo is typing.

MERCUTIO

Any keyboard warrior can snap back with a reply.

BENVOLIO

Nah, fam, Romeo's gonna hit him up and say if he's down to duel
or not.

MERCUTIO

RIP Romeo, bruh. Dude's already down bad. Got his heart left on
read. Now he has to throw hands with Tybalt?

BENVOLIO

And what's the big deal with Tybalt?

MERCUTIO

Dude's a beast, like the Prince of Cats. His style is textbook. He's
got mad finesse, sick timing, and can close the distance in a flash,
he is patient and has a mean combo. He's the slickest, can thread
a needle in a brawl. The GOAT of dueling, schooled by masters
in the art of the sword. He's got all the moves down, from the
classic passado to the sneaky reverso, and finishes with the stinger
that never misses.

BENVOLIO

The what?

MERCUTIO

The pox of such antic, lisping, affecting fantasticoes; these new tuners of accents! 'By Jesu, a very good blade! a very tall man! a very good whore!' Why, is not this a lamentable thing, grandsire, that we should be thus afflicted with these strange flies, these fashion-mongers, these perdona-mi's, who stand so much on the new form, that they cannot at ease on the old bench? O, their bones, their bones!

*(Enter **Romeo**)*

BENVOLIO

Here comes Romeo, here comes Romeo.

MERCUTIO

Without his roe, like a dried herring: flesh, flesh, how art thou fishified! Now is he for the numbers that Petrarch flowed in: Laura to his lady was but a kitchen-wench; marry, she had a better love to be-rhyme her; Dido a dowdy; Cleopatra a gipsy; Helen and Hero hildings and harlots; Thisbe a grey eye or so, but not to the purpose. Signior Romeo, bon jour! there's a French salutation to your French slop. You gave us the counterfeit fairly last night.

ROMEO

Good morrow to you both. What counterfeit did I give you?

BENVOLIO

The what now?

MERCUTIO

Man, I'm so over these try-hard posers, with their fancy pants lingo. Always so extra. When they're all, "This sword? Cray cray." "This dude? A Chad." "That lady? A thoty." Like, can we not? Why we gotta deal with these wannabes, these try hards, flexing their weird slang, so caught up in their finesse they can't even chill without making a scene, like "blud, my fit is flames bruv"!"

(**Romeo** *makes his entrance*)

BENVOLIO

Yo, look alive, here comes your boy, Romeo!

MERCUTIO

My dude's looking slim, like a dried-up old fish. Bro's all pail and hungry, now he is ready for some love songs. But all those baddies from the songs are basic compared to his bae. Joline is so old, Delilah is stuck in NYC, a thousand miles away, and Billy Jean is a stage 3 clinger. Caroline was pretty sweet, but who really cares? Yo, Romeo, what's good? Or a French "bonjour" to ya, to go with those saggy joggers you're rocking. You ghosted us hard last night, fam!

ROMEO

What's good? What do you mean I ghosted?

MERCUTIO

The ship, sir, the slip; can you not conceive?

ROMEO

Pardon, good Mercutio, my business was great; and in such a case as mine a man may strain courtesy.

MERCUTIO

That's as much as to say, such a case as yours constrains a man to bow in the hams.

ROMEO

Meaning, to court'sy.

MERCUTIO

Thou hast most kindly hit it.

ROMEO

A most courteous exposition.

MERCUTIO

Nay, I am the very pink of courtesy.

MERCUTIO

Bro, you bailed. Don't cap.

ROMEO

My B, Mercutio. Had to handle some biz. It was so important I forgot my manners.

MERCUTIO

You mean to say your "important biz" was getting busy.

ROMEO

You mean smash?

MERCUTIO

Deadass bro.

ROMEO

Nice... real smooth, very mature.

MERCUTIO

Facts, I am the pink flower-the master, of maturity and manners.

ROMEO

Pink for flower.

MERCUTIO

Right.

ROMEO

Why, then is my pump well flowered.

MERCUTIO

Well said: follow me this jest now till thou hast worn out thy pump, that when the single sole of it is worn, the jest may remain after the wearing sole singular.

ROMEO

O single-soled jest, solely singular for the singleness.

MERCUTIO

Come between us, good Benvolio; my wits faint.

ROMEO

Switch and spurs, switch and spurs; or I'll cry a match.

ROMEO

Pink flower?

MERCUTIO

Facts.

ROMEO

Well, my dog loves sniffing pink flowers.

MERCUTIO

A'ight, that sent me. But you better feed your dog before he runs off and leaves you with just your jokes. Looks like he is just skin and bones.

ROMEO

Trash, that was straight up corny.

MERCUTIO

Help me out Benvolio, he is roasting me.

ROMEO

Nope, keep it going, or I'll claim the W.

MERCUTIO

Nay, if thy wits run the wild-goose chase, I have done, for thou hast more of the wild-goose in one of thy wits than, I am sure, I have in my whole five: was I with you there for the goose?

ROMEO

Thou wast never with me for any thing when thou wast not there for the goose.

MERCUTIO

I will bite thee by the ear for that jest.

ROMEO

Nay, good goose, bite not.

MERCUTIO

Thy wit is a very bitter sweeting; it is a most sharp sauce.

ROMEO

And is it not well served in to a sweet goose?

MERCUTIO

O here's a wit of cheveril, that stretches from an inch narrow to an ell broad!

MERCUTIO

Dude, I can't out roast you, no cap. One of your comebacks slaps harder than five of mine. Was I even close this time?

ROMEO

You're just not on my level, baby girl.

MERCUTIO

I'll bite your ear off for that!

ROMEO

Chill, baby girl, don't snack on my ear. I might like it.

MERCUTIO

Your burns are so spicy! Sometimes zesty.

ROMEO

Well, isn't that how my baby girl likes it?

MERCUTIO

Okay, you stretched this joke as far as it will go.

ROMEO

I stretch it out for that word 'broad;' which added to the goose, proves thee far and wide a broad goose.

MERCUTIO

Why, is not this better now than groaning for love? Now art thou sociable, now art thou Romeo; now art thou what thou art, by art as well as by nature: for this drivelling love is like a great natural, that runs lolling up and down to hide his bauble in a hole.

BENVOLIO

Stop there, stop there.

MERCUTIO

Thou desirest me to stop in my tale against the hair.

BENVOLIO

Thou wouldst else have made thy tale large.

MERCUTIO

O, thou art deceived; I would have made it short: for I was come to the whole depth of my tale; and meant, indeed, to occupy the argument no longer.

ROMEO

Here's goodly gear!

ROMEO

My joke is stretched thin? That means your joke is still thicc.
That makes you my fat baby girl.

MERCUTIO

But frfr, isn't this roasting better than simping over some chick?
Now you're vibing, now you're the real Romeo. You're finally the
Romeo you're meant to be, no cap. Your simping turned you into
a whiny little baby looking for someone to play with his toy.

BENVOLIO

Yo, get off the gas Mercutio.

MERCUTIO

Stop my tale before its finished?

BENVOLIO

Your tale was getting too long.

MERCUTIO

Nah, you got it twisted. I was gonna wrap it up, had nearly reached
the peak, and was 'bout to finish.

ROMEO

See, now that was God tier!

*(Enter **nurse** and **Peter**)*

MERCUTIO

A sail, a sail!

BENVOLIO

Two, two; a shirt and a smock.

NURSE

Peter!

PETER

Anon!

NURSE

My fan, Peter.

MERCUTIO

Good Peter, to hide her face; for her fan's the fairer face.

NURSE

God ye good morrow, gentlemen.

*(The **nurse** rolls in with her servant, **Peter**)*

MERCUTIO

Oh, snap! A blimp, a blimp!

BENVOLIO

What a match these two are.

NURSE

Peter!

PETER

Sup?

NURSE

Hand over my fan.

MERCUTIO

Aye, Peter, give her the fan so she can cover her face. Her fan's slaying compared to that mug.

NURSE

Top of the morn to ya, lads.

MERCUTIO

God ye good den, fair gentlewoman.

NURSE

Is it good den?

MERCUTIO

'Tis no less, I tell you, for the bawdy hand of the dial is now upon the prick of noon.

NURSE

Out upon you! what a man are you!

MERCUTIO

One, gentlewoman, that God hath made for himself to mar.

NURSE

By my troth, it is well said; 'for himself to mar,' quoth a'? Gentlemen, can any of you tell me where I may find the young Romeo?

ROMEO

I can tell you; but young Romeo will be older when you have found him than he was when you sought him: I am the youngest of that name, for fault of a worse.

MERCUTIO

Yas queen, good afternoon!

NURSE

Is it afternoon already?

MERCUTIO

Yup, the thicc hand of the clock's pointing straight up.

NURSE

Ick, dude! What's wrong with you?

MERCUTIO

I'm just a dude, ma'am, whom the big guy upstairs built for epic fails.

NURSE

Deadass, that's facts! "Built for epic fails." Yo, can any of you guys point me to young Romeo?

ROMEO

Say less, but young Romeo's gonna level up in age by the time you slide into his DMs. I'm the youngest Romeo in town, I don't know a Romeo as young and bad as I.

NURSE

You say well.

MERCUTIO

Yea, is the worst well? very well took, i' faith; wisely, wisely.

NURSE

If you be he, sir, I desire some confidence with you.

BENVOLIO

She will indite him to some supper.

MERCUTIO

A bawd, a bawd, a bawd! so ho!

ROMEO

What hast thou found?

NURSE

You've got bars.

MERCUTIO

Is bad even lit? I'll give it to you...

NURSE

*(To **Romeo**)* If you be he, sir, I'll slide into your DMs.

BENVOLIO

She's gonna slide him an invite to a feast I bet.

MERCUTIO

A Player! A Player! I see you!

ROMEO

What's good?

MERCUTIO

No hare, sir; unless a hare, sir, in a lenten pie, that is something stale and hoar ere it be spent.

(Sings)

"An old hare hoar, and an old hare hoar, is very good meat in lent but a hare that is hoar is too much for a score, when it hoars ere it be spent."

Romeo, will you come to your father's? We'll to dinner, thither.

ROMEO

I will follow you.

MERCUTIO

Farewell, ancient lady; farewell,

(Singing 'lady, lady, lady.')

*(Exeunt **Mercutio** and **Benvolio**)*

NURSE

Marry, farewell! I pray you, sir, what saucy merchant was this, that was so full of his ropery?

ROMEO

A gentleman, nurse, that loves to hear himself talk, and will speak more in a minute than he will stand to in a month.

MERCUTIO

She ain't a thot, unless she's that busted AND she is easy.

(He struts and hums)"An old hare hoar, and an old hare hoar, is very good meat in lent, but a hare that is hoar is too much for a score, when it hoars ere it be spent."

(Speaking) Romeo, you hitting up your dad's crib for some grub? Let's roll.

ROMEO

I'll catch up with you.

MERCUTIO

Peace out, boomer. Later, gator.

*(Exit **Benvolio** and **Mercutio**)*

NURSE

Who's that loudmouth troll dropping' vulgar jokes?

ROMEO

Oh, he's just a bro in love with his own voice. Dude types faster than he reads.

NURSE

An a' speak any thing against me, I'll take him down, an a' were lustier than he is, and twenty such Jacks; and if I cannot, I'll find those that shall. Scurvy knave! I am none of his flirt-gills; I am none of his skains-mates. And thou must stand by too, and suffer every knave to use me at his pleasure?

PETER

I saw no man use you a pleasure; if I had, my weapon should quickly have been out, I warrant you: I dare draw as soon as another man, if I see occasion in a good quarrel, and the law on my side.

NURSE

Now, afore God, I am so vexed, that every part about me quivers. Scurvy knave! Pray you, sir, a word: and as I told you, my young lady bade me inquire you out; what she bade me say, I will keep to myself: but first let me tell ye, if ye should lead her into a fool's paradise, as they say, it were a very gross kind of behavior, as they say: for the gentlewoman is young; and, therefore, if you should deal double with her, truly it were an ill thing to be offered to any gentlewoman, and very weak dealing.

ROMEO

Nurse, commend me to thy lady and mistress. I protest unto thee-

NURSE

Good heart, and, i' faith, I will tell her as much: Lord, Lord, she will be a joyful woman.

NURSE

If he wants to roast me, he better be ready to catch these hands, even if he rolls deep with a squad. I'll call in some backup. That dirty rat! I'm not one of his lil hoes. I'm not one of his lil punk friends. *(To **Peter**)* And you're just going to sit back and let him roast me?

PETER

Wasn't no one roasting you. If I heard that, I'd be ready to throw down some justice real quick.

NURSE

I'm so shook right now; swear it's got me all kinds of heated! That dude's toxic! *(To **Romeo**)* But listen, my girl slid into my DMs to find you. What she said, I'm keeping on the DL for now. So, listen – if you're playing her, that's straight-up villainy, she's just a chile. Don't be doing her dirty, it's a bad look, frfr.

ROMEO

Nurse, shoot my best to your lady. On the real, I-

NURSE

You're solid, I get it. And she'll be all heart eyes when I spill. She's gonna be living her best life.

ROMEO

What wilt thou tell her, nurse? thou dost not mark me.

NURSE

I will tell her, sir, that you do protest; which, as I take it, is a gentlemanlike offer.

ROMEO

Bid her devise some means to come to shrift this afternoon; and there she shall at Friar Laurence' cell be shrived and married. Here is for thy pains.

NURSE

No truly sir; not a penny.

ROMEO

Go to; I say you shall.

NURSE

This afternoon, sir? Well, she shall be there.

ROMEO

And stay, good nurse, behind the abbey wall: within this hour my man shall be with thee and bring thee cords made like a tackled stair; which to the high top-gallant of my joy must be my convoy in

ROMEO

Hold up, what are you actually gonna tell her, nurse? You're tripping me out.

NURSE

Bruh, I'll spill that you're down on one knee, like a #Gentleman.

ROMEO

A'ight, tell her to cook up some alibi to dip from her crib and hit up the abbey later. At Friar Laurence's spot, she can give a confession and we can lock it down. *(Handing her coins)* This is for keeping it one hundred.

NURSE

Nah, for real, I don't need your money.

ROMEO

Frfr, take it.

NURSE

(Bet, taking the money) Tonight? She's down.

ROMEO

Hang tight nurse. I'll have someone from my squad meet you behind the chapel with a rope ladder in about an hour. I'm gonna yeet over the wall tonight and use the rope ladder to get into her

the secret night. Farewell; be trusty, and I'll quit thy pains: farewell; commend me to thy mistress.

NURSE

Now God in heaven bless thee! Hark you, sir.

ROMEO

What say'st thou, my dear nurse?

NURSE

Is your man secret? Did you ne'er hear say, two may keep counsel, putting one away?

ROMEO

I warrant thee, my man's as true as steel.

NURSE

Well, sir; my mistress is the sweetest lady--Lord, Lord! when 'twas a little prating thing:--O, there is a nobleman in town, one Paris, that would fain lay knife aboard; but she, good soul, had as lief see a toad, a very toad, as see him. I anger her sometimes and tell her that Paris is the properer man; but, I'll warrant you, when I say so, she looks as pale as any clout in the versal world. Doth not rosemary and Romeo begin both with a letter?

room, then it's just me and Juliet, on the low. Catch you later. Stay valid. Hype me up to your queen, a'ight?

NURSE

Bless up from the heavens... wait hold up!

ROMEO

What's good, Nurse?

NURSE

Can your bro keep that on the DL? Ever heard of, "snitches get stiches"?

ROMEO

Trust, my guy can hold it down.

NURSE

Okay, listen, my girl's heart is bussin, frfr. Like, there's this dude, Paris, thinks he's all that, but Juliet just swipes left every time. I troll her sometimes, saying he's got more rizz than you. Swear, she goes pale as a ghost. Ain't it funny both "Rosemary" and "Romeo" start with an R?

ROMEO

Ay, nurse; what of that? both with an R.

NURSE

Ah. mocker! that's the dog's name; R is for the--No; I know it begins with some other letter:--and she hath the prettiest sententious of it, of you and rosemary, that it would do you good to hear it.

ROMEO

Commend me to thy lady.

NURSE

Ay, a thousand times. Peter!

PETER

Anon!

NURSE

Peter, take my fan, and go before and apace.

(Exeunt)

ORIGINAL TEXT

ROMEO

Yeah, so? They both start with R.

NURSE

LOL, you're a savage— a straight-up dog. But real talk, she's got nothing but mad feels for you and that Rosemary.

ROMEO

Slide my love to your girl.

NURSE

Oh, I'm gonna put it on blast, for sure. Peter!

PETER

Locked and loaded.

NURSE

*(Handoff, giving **Peter** her fan)* Lessgo, fam. Peace out.

(Exit all)

ACT TWO

SCENE FIVE

(Enter Juliet)

JULIET

The clock struck nine when I did send the nurse; in half an hour she promised to return. perchance she cannot meet him: that's not so. O, she is lame! love's heralds should be thoughts, which ten times faster glide than the sun's beams, driving back shadows over louring hills: therefore do nimble-pinion'd doves draw love, and therefore hath the wind-swift Cupid wings. Now is the sun upon the highmost hill of this day's journey, and from nine till twelve is three long hours, yet she is not come. Had she affections and warm youthful blood, she would be as swift in motion as a ball; my words would bandy her to my sweet love, and his to me: but old folks, many feign as they were dead; unwieldy, slow, heavy and pale as lead. O God, she comes!

(Enter nurse and Peter)

O honey nurse, what news? Hast thou met with him? Send thy man away.

NURSE

Peter, stay at the gate.

ACT TWO

SCENE FIVE

(Juliet enters)

JULIET

I sent the nurse at like nine. Maybe she can't find him? No way. Ugh, she's so slow! Love's DMs should hit like thoughts, dropping notifs faster than a reel of the sunrise chasing away the past. Strong enough to yeet the shadows over the hills. Just like Venus whipping through the sky on the wings of doves. That's how Cupids so fast bruh, his wings. Now it's noon, it's been 3 whole hours and she's MIA. If she was vibing with a hot young bro, she'd be bouncing back faster than a pickleball. But these boomers are like zombies, no cap – stiff, slow, dragging. OMG, she's here!

(The nurse and Peter enter)

OMG, OMG, Spill! Did you chat with him? Peter, bounce for a sec.

NURSE

Peter, chill over there.

*(Exit **Peter**)*

JULIET

Now, good sweet nurse,--O Lord, why look'st thou sad? Though news be sad, yet tell them merrily; if good, thou shamest the music of sweet news by playing it to me with so sour a face.

NURSE

I am a-weary, give me leave awhile: fie, how my bones ache! what a jaunt have I had!

JULIET

I would thou hadst my bones, and I thy news: nay, come, I pray thee, speak; good, good nurse, speak.

NURSE

Jesu, what haste? can you not stay awhile? Do you not see that I am out of breath?

JULIET

How art thou out of breath, when thou hast breath to say to me that thou art out of breath? The excuse that thou dost make in this delay is longer than the tale thou dost excuse. Is thy news good, or bad? answer to that; say either, and I'll stay the circumstance: let me be satisfied, is't good or bad?

*(**Peter** exits)*

JULIET

Nurse, what's with the sad filter? If the news is all tears, keep it a hundred. But if it's all good, you're killing the vibe with that sus look.

NURSE

Guurl, I'm beat, let me catch my breath. My whole body's screaming fam! I been all over the place.

JULIET

I wish you'd match my energy and give me the update. C'mon, please, spill it, good nurse!

NURSE

Girl, pause. Don't you see I'm straight-up gassed? What's the rush anyway?

JULIET

How can you be gassed and still have the air to say you're gassed? You're taking longer to make excuses than it would take to spill. Frfr just say if it's good news or bad, and I'll wait for the deets. I need to know – is it a vibe or naur?

NURSE

Well, you have made a simple choice; you know not how to choose a man: Romeo! no, not he; though his face be better than any man's, yet his leg excels all men's; and for a hand, and a foot, and a body, though they be not to be talked on, yet they are past compare: he is not the flower of courtesy, but, I'll warrant him, as gentle as a lamb. Go thy ways, wench; serve God. What, have you dined at home?

JULIET

No, no: but all this did I know before. What says he of our marriage? What of that?

NURSE

Lord, how my head aches! what a head have I! It beats as it would fall in twenty pieces. My back o' t' other side,--O, my back, my back! Beshrew your heart for sending me about, to catch my death with jaunting up and down!

JULIET

I' faith, I am sorry that thou art not well. Sweet, sweet, sweet nurse, tell me, what says my love?

NURSE

Your love says, like an honest gentleman, and a courteous, and a kind, and a handsome, and, I warrant, a virtuous,--Where is your mother?

NURSE

Girl, your choices are sus. You don't know how to pick 'em.
Romeo? Seriously? Okay, so he is fine, and has some rizz, but his
body is lackin. Still, low-key, he is kind of cute. He's not the most
polite, but trust, he's a total softie and he's pretty chill. Anyway,
you do you, boo. Have you eaten yet?

JULIET

Nope, haven't eaten. You're not telling me want I want to know!
Spill - what's the deal with our marriage? I need the update!

NURSE

Ugh, my head's straight thumping, girl! Feels like it's gonna
explode into a billion pieces. And my back, oh -*(Juliet rubs her
back)* ooh right there my back is paining! You're wrong for
making me your errand girl. I could literally die!

JULIET

I feel bad you're low key dying and all, but nurse! What did my
bae say?

NURSE

Your guy is legit a chill bro, kind vibes, charming, looking like a
snack - and yeah, valid frfr. But wait, where's your mom at?

JULIET

Where is my mother! why, she is within; where should she be?
How oddly thou repliest! 'Your love says, like an honest
gentleman, where is your mother?'

NURSE

O God's lady dear! Are you so hot? Marry, come up, I trow; is
this the poultice for my aching bones? Henceforward do your
messages yourself.

JULIET

Here's such a coil! come, what says Romeo?

NURSE

Have you got leave to go to shrift to-day?

JULIET

I have.

NURSE

Then hie you hence to Friar Laurence' cell; there stays a husband
to make you a wife: now comes the wanton blood up in your
cheeks, they'll be in scarlet straight at any news. hie you to church;
I must another way, to fetch a ladder, by the which your love must
climb a bird's nest soon when it is dark: I am the drudge and toil

JULIET

Where's my mom? She's around, where she always is? Why are you coming at me weird? "Your boo's like a good dude or whatever, where's your mom?"

NURSE

Chill! You're being all kinds of extra rn. Is this drama gonna cure my aching back? Nope! Slide into his DMs yourself from now on!

JULIET

Nurse, you're doing too much. Just tell me –what's up with Romeo?

NURSE

You got the green light to go drop a confession today?

JULIET

Yeah, I did.

NURSE

Then get over to Friar Laurence's pad. Your man's waiting to put a ring on it. I see you going all rosy-cheeked at the mere mention. Get to the church. I'm off to snag a rope ladder, so your man can smash that like button IRL, while the moon is out. Here I am, working like your hype woman, and you – you're about to be

in your delight, but you shall bear the burden soon at night. Go;
I'll to dinner: hie you to the cell.

JULIET

Hie to high fortune! Honest nurse, farewell.

(Exeunt)

working on wifey duties through the night. Peace out, I'm hitting the deli. You dash to Friar Laurence's spot.

JULIET

Cross your fingers for me. Big thanks, nurse!

(They exit)

ACT TWO

SCENE SIX

*(Enter **Friar Laurence** and **Romeo**)*

FRIAR LAURENCE

So smile the heavens upon this holy act, that after hours with sorrow chide us not!

ROMEO

Amen, amen! but come what sorrow can, it cannot countervail the exchange of joy that one short minute gives me in her sight: do thou but close our hands with holy words, then love-devouring death do what he dare; it is enough I may but call her mine.

FRIAR LAURENCE

These violent delights have violent ends and in their triumph die, like fire and powder, which as they kiss consume: the sweetest honey is loathsome in his own deliciousness and in the taste confounds the appetite: therefore love moderately; long love doth so; too swift arrives as tardy as too slow.

*(Enter **Juliet**)*

Here comes the lady: O, so light a foot will ne'er wear out the everlasting flint: a lover may bestride the gossamer that idles in the wanton summer air, and yet not fall; so light is vanity.

ACT TWO

SCENE SIX

*(**Friar Laurence** and **Romeo** enter)*

FRIAR LAURENCE

Hope the stars are vibing with our union so we don't catch any
bad feels later.

ROMEO

Big facts, big facts! But let's roll with it, no drama can kill the vibe
she brings, just one minute with her is pure bliss: do your thing,
link us with those sacred words, then whatever comes next, we're
here for it. Just to call her my girl is #Goals.

FRIAR LAURENCE

Yo, intense feels can have intense endings, they can blow up just
like when fire meets gunpowder. It's all fireworks, but too much
of a good thing can be a buzzkill. So love chill, not too fast or slow
– steady wins the race.

*(Enter **Juliet,** she rushes in and hugs **Romeo**)*

Here she is, stepping so much lighter than air, her head lives in
the clouds. Lovers so light they can dance on a spiderwebs in the
breeze without falling, man loves a trip!

JULIET

Good even to my ghostly confessor.

FRIAR LAURENCE

Romeo shall thank thee, daughter, for us both.

JULIET

As much to him, else is his thanks too much.

ROMEO

Ah, Juliet, if the measure of thy joy be heap'd like mine and that thy skill be more to blazon it, then sweeten with thy breath this neighbour air, and let rich music's tongue unfold the imagined happiness that both receive in either by this dear encounter.

JULIET

Conceit, more rich in matter than in words, brags of his substance, not of ornament: they are but beggars that can count their worth; but my true love is grown to such excess I cannot sum up sum of half my wealth.

FRIAR LAURENCE

Come, come with me, and we will make short work; for, by your leaves, you shall not stay alone till holy church incorporate two in one.

(Exeunt)

JULIET

What's good, my holy bro?

FRIAR LAURENCE

Romeo's throwing thanks your way, from both of us, fam.

JULIET

I'll hit him back with the same energy, to keep it one hundred.

ROMEO

Ah, Juliet, if your vibes are as lit as mine, and if you got better bars than me, spit me a verse about how happy we'll be.

JULIET

I've got love that slaps harder than words can describe. Anyone who's counting their blessings is down bad compared to me. My love's got me feeling so blessed, I couldn't even count half of 'em.

FRIAR LAURENCE

Let's get moving and seal the deal. Obvie, I can't leave you two alone until you're united in marriage.

(They exit.)

ACT THREE

SCENE ONE

*(Enter **Mercutio**, **Benvolio**, Page, and Servants)*

BENVOLIO

I pray thee, good Mercutio, let's retire: the day is hot, the Capulets abroad, and, if we meet, we shall not scape a brawl; for now, these hot days, is the mad blood stirring.

MERCUTIO

Thou art like one of those fellows that when he enters the confines of a tavern claps me his sword upon the table and says 'God send me no need of thee!' and by the operation of the second cup draws it on the drawer, when indeed there is no need.

BENVOLIO

Am I like such a fellow?

MERCUTIO

Come, come, thou art as hot a Jack in thy mood as any in Italy, and as soon moved to be moody, and as soon moody to be moved.

ACT THREE

SCENE ONE

*(**Mercutio**, his page, and **Benvolio** enter with their squad)*

BENVOLIO

Mercutio, my guy, let's cut our losses and jet. The day is scorched, and the Capulet crew is on the prowl. Cross paths and we'll for sure be throwing hands, this heat's got everyone on edge.

MERCUTIO

Bro, you're like that guy who, after one brewski, slams his steel on the bar and is all like, "Hope I won't need this." But by the bottom of the next, he's draws it on the bartender when indeed there is no need.

BENVOLIO

You saying I'm that guy?

MERCUTIO

Bruh, you're spicier than an Italian having a bad day, quick to get shook and you'll find any excuse to start swinging.

BENVOLIO

And what to?

MERCUTIO

Nay, an there were two such, we should have none shortly, for
one would kill the other. Thou! why, thou wilt quarrel with a man
that hath a hair more, or a hair less, in his beard, than thou hast:
thou wilt quarrel with a man for cracking nuts, having no other
reason but because thou hast hazel eyes: what eye but such an eye
would spy out such a quarrel? Thy head is as fun of quarrels as an
egg is full of meat, and yet thy head hath been beaten as addle as
an egg for quarrelling: thou hast quarrelled with a man for
coughing in the street, because he hath wakened thy dog that hath
lain asleep in the sun: didst thou not fall out with a tailor for
wearing his new doublet before Easter? with another, for tying his
new shoes with old riband? and yet thou wilt tutor me from
quarrelling!

BENVOLIO

An I were so apt to quarrel as thou art, any man should buy the
fee-simple of my life for an hour and a quarter.

MERCUTIO

The fee-simple! O simple!

BENVOLIO

By my head, here come the Capulets.

(Enter **Tybalt** and others)

BENVOLIO

Your point being?

MERCUTIO

If there were two of you, RIP 'cause you'd end each other. You'd scrap with a guy over his beard being one hair too many or too few. Or if some guy is cracking nuts and looks at you sideways because, what, you got green eyes? It's wild, man. Your noggin's packed with more reasons to fight than an omelet has eggs, but it's all scrambled from the brawls. Didn't you get into it with a guy for just waking up your dog? And you tried to go toe-to-toe with your tailor over sporting a fresh fit too early in the season? And with another for rocking new kicks with vintage laces? Yet here you are, schooling me on how to chill? Please!

BENVOLIO

If I picked fights like you, I'd be shelling out mad bread for life insurance.

MERCUTIO

Life insurance? Calm down!

BENVOLIO

Great, the Capulets just rolled in.

(Tybalt, Petruchio, and the Capulets show up)

MERCUTIO

By my heel, I care not.

TYBALT

Follow me close, for I will speak to them. Gentlemen, good den: a word with one of you.

MERCUTIO

And but one word with one of us? couple it with something; make it a word and a blow.

TYBALT

You shall find me apt enough to that, sir, an you will give me occasion.

MERCUTIO

Could you not take some occasion without giving?

TYBALT

Mercutio, thou consort'st with Romeo,--

MERCUTIO

Consort! what, dost thou make us minstrels? An thou make minstrels of us, look to hear nothing but discords: here's my fiddlestick; here's that shall make you dance. 'Zounds, consort!

MERCUTIO

And I'm supposed to care, why?

TYBALT

Stay close, I wanna holla at them. *(To the **Montagues**)* Sup, gents. Let's have a quick talk.

MERCUTIO

You want a word with us? Make it worth our while. Throw down a challenge.

TYBALT

Trust, you'll find me ready if you want to start something.

MERCUTIO

Can't you cook up some beef without me seasoning it?

TYBALT

Thou rolls with Romeo, no?

MERCUTIO

"Roll with?" What, you reckon we're a band? If we strike a chord, it's gonna be chaos, trust! *(Grasps his sword)* This is my axe, and trust me, I'll play a banger for you with it. "Come on!"

BENVOLIO

We talk here in the public haunt of men: either withdraw unto some private place, and reason coldly of your grievances, or else depart; here all eyes gaze on us.

MERCUTIO

Men's eyes were made to look, and let them gaze; I will not budge for no man's pleasure.

*(Enter **Romeo**)*

TYBALT

Well, peace be with you, sir: here comes my man.

MERCUTIO

But I'll be hanged, sir, if he wear your livery: marry, go before to field, he'll be your follower; your worship in that sense may call him 'man.'

TYBALT

Romeo, the hate I bear thee can afford no better term than this,-- thou art a villain.

BENVOLIO

We're out in the open, man. Take it somewhere private, or just chill. We got eyes on us here.

MERCUTIO

Bro's eyes were made to look, let them throw some side eyes. I will not budge for no man!

*(**Romeo** enters)*

TYBALT

Well, peace be with you, sir. Here comes my man now.

MERCUTIO

He ain't your man. If he follows you around like a lost puppy, then maybe he's your "man."

TYBALT

Romeo, I don't know what else to say to you besides you're straight trash bro!

ROMEO

Tybalt, the reason that I have to love thee doth much excuse the appertaining rage to such a greeting: villain am I none; therefore farewell; I see thou know'st me not.

TYBALT

Boy, this shall not excuse the injuries that thou hast done me; therefore turn and draw.

ROMEO

I do protest, I never injured thee, but love thee better than thou canst devise, till thou shalt know the reason of my love: and so, good Capulet,--which name I tender ss dearly as my own,--be satisfied.

MERCUTIO

O calm, dishonourable, vile submission! Alla stoccata carries it away. (Draws) Tybalt, you rat-catcher, will you walk?

TYBALT

What wouldst thou have with me?

ROMEO

Tybalt, the mad love I have for you totally excuses the rage I feel from such a greeting. Trash I'm not. Therefore, peace out! I see thou doesn't know me at all!

TYBALT

Bruh, you really thought we wouldn't notice? Though I was gonna let it slide? Guess again! Now turn and draw!

ROMEO

Nay, man. I never did you dirty! There's love between us deeper than you know. And no cap, I respect the name Capulet like it's my own.

MERCUTIO

This sweet talk is straight-up disgraceful! Let's see if your blade speaks as sweetly! *(Unsheathes his sword)* Tybalt, you ready to dance or what?

TYBALT

Bro, what do you want from me?

MERCUTIO

Good king of cats, nothing but one of your nine lives; that I mean to make bold withal, and as you shall use me hereafter, drybeat the rest of the eight. Will you pluck your sword out of his pitcher by the ears? make haste, lest mine be about your ears ere it be out.

TYBALT

I am for you. *(Drawing)*

ROMEO

Gentle Mercutio, put thy rapier up.

MERCUTIO

Come, sir, your passado. *(They fight)*

ROMEO

Draw, Benvolio; beat down their weapons. Gentlemen, for shame, forbear this outrage! Tybalt, Mercutio, the prince expressly hath forbidden bandying in Verona streets: hold, Tybalt! good Mercutio!

*(**Tybalt** under **Romeo's** arm stabs **Mercutio**)*

PETRUCHIO

Away, Tybalt.

MERCUTIO

Good King of Cats, I just want one of your nine lives! Get that sword out, or you'll feel mine by your ear before yours even swings!

TYBALT

Say less! Let's go! *(Draws his sword)*

ROMEO

Yo, Mercutio, sheath your blade bro!

MERCUTIO

*(To **Tybalt**)* Alright, bring it! Show me what you got!

ROMEO

(Grabs his sword) Benvolio, help me break them up! Boys, cut this nonsense! The prince banned this from the streets! Stop, Tybalt! Ease up, Mercutio!

*(As **Romeo** tries to stop the brawl, **Tybalt** stabs **Mercutio** under **Romeo's** arm)*

PETRUCHIO

Tybalt we gotta bounce!

*(Exeunt **Tybalt**, **Petruchio**, and the other **Capulets**)*

MERCUTIO

I am hurt. A plague o' both your houses! I am sped. Is he gone, and hath nothing?

BENVOLIO

What, art thou hurt?

MERCUTIO

Ay, ay, a scratch, a scratch; marry, 'tis enough. Where is my page? Go, villain, fetch a surgeon.

*(Exit **Page**)*

ROMEO

Courage, man; the hurt cannot be much.

MERCUTIO

No, 'tis not so deep as a well, nor so wide as a church-door; but 'tis enough,'twill serve: ask for me to-morrow, and you shall find me a grave man. I am peppered, I warrant, for this world. A plague o' both your houses! 'Zounds, a dog, a rat, a mouse, a cat, to scratch a man to death! a braggart, a rogue, a villain, that fights by the book of arithmetic! Why the devil came you between us? I was hurt under your arm.

(Tybalt, Petruchio, and the Capulets dip out)

MERCUTIO

I'm hit! A curse on both your houses! I'm toast. Is he gone? I
didn't get him?

BENVOLIO

You good, bro?

MERCUTIO

It's just a flesh wound, but it'll do. Yo, page! Grab the doc!

(Mercutio's page exits)

ROMEO

Stay strong, it's not that serious.

MERCUTIO

Nay, it ain't too deep or wide, but it's a done deal. Hit me up
tomorrow and you'll find me in a grave! Damn it all, both your
fams can catch this curse! Done in by a scrub! Why the devil did
you come between us? I was hurt under your arm!

ROMEO

I thought all for the best.

MERCUTIO

Help me into some house, Benvolio, or I shall faint. A plague o'
both your houses! They have made worms' meat of me: I have it,
and soundly too: your houses!

*(Exeunt **Mercutio** and **Benvolio**)*

ROMEO

This gentleman, the prince's near ally, my very friend, hath got his
mortal hurt in my behalf; my reputation stain'd with Tybalt's
slander,--Tybalt, that an hour hath been my kinsman! O sweet
Juliet, thy beauty hath made me effeminate and in my temper
soften'd valour's steel!

*(Re-enter **Benvolio**)*

BENVOLIO

O Romeo, Romeo, brave Mercutio's dead! That gallant spirit hath
aspired the clouds, which too untimely here did scorn the earth.

ROMEO

This day's black fate on more days doth depend; this but begins
the woe, others must end.

ROMEO

I only meant to do right...

MERCUTIO

Get me indoors, Benvolio, I'm 'bout to black out. Both your cribs can catch this curse for real! They turned me into worm chow. I'm out!

*(**Mercutio** and **Benvolio** bounce)*

ROMEO

Mercutio was kin to the prince and my ride or die, got taken out standing up to Tybalt for me—Tybalt, who's just become my family! Juliet, your love's turned me soft, dulled my fighter's edge!

*(**Benvolio** comes back)*

BENVOLIO

Bro, Romeo, Mercutio's gone! His bold spirit's taken flight, way before its time!

ROMEO

What's gone down today is just the start. It's gonna bring a world of hurt!

BENVOLIO

Here comes the furious Tybalt back again.

*(Re-enter **Tybalt**)*

ROMEO

Alive, in triumph! and Mercutio slain! Away to heaven, respective lenity, and fire-eyed fury be my conduct now! Now, Tybalt, take the villain back again, that late thou gavest me; for Mercutio's soul is but a little way above our heads, staying for thine to keep him company: either thou, or I, or both, must go with him.

TYBALT

Thou, wretched boy, that didst consort him here, shalt with him hence.

ROMEO

This shall determine that.

*(They fight; **Tybalt** falls)*

BENVOLIO

Romeo, away, be gone! The citizens are up, and Tybalt slain. Stand not amazed: the prince will doom thee death, if thou art taken: hence, be gone, away!

ROMEO

O, I am fortune's fool!

BENVOLIO

And look who's back—Tybalt, looking for more.

*(**Tybalt** enters again)*

ROMEO

He is strutting around, and Mercutio's dead? This ain't it fam, No more playing nice! Tybalt, you wanted the smoke, you got it! Mercutio's spirit's barely gone, and it's waiting on you! It's you or me, Tybalt! One of us joins him!

TYBALT

You're done, Romeo! You chilled with him; now you'll follow him out!

ROMEO

Let's see!

*(They scrap. **Tybalt** gets murked)*

BENVOLIO

Romeo, you gotta dip! People are watching, and Tybalt's out. The prince will have you clapped if they catch you! Bounce, now!

ROMEO

Man, fates got it out for me...

BENVOLIO

Why dost thou stay?

*(Exit **Romeo**)*

(Enter the watch)

CITIZEN OF THE WATCH

Which way ran he that kill'd Mercutio? Tybalt, that murderer, which way ran he?

BENVOLIO

There lies that Tybalt.

CITIZEN OF THE WATCH

Up, sir, go with me; I charge thee in the princes name, obey.

*(Enter **prince**, attended; **Montague, Capulet**, their Wives, and others)*

PRINCE

Where are the vile beginners of this fray?

BENVOLIO

Why are you still here?

*(**Romeo** leaves.)*

(The watch shows up)

CITIZEN OF THE WATCH

Who offed Mercutio? Where'd Tybalt the killer, go?

BENVOLIO

Tybalt's right there, taking a permanent nap.

CITIZEN OF THE WATCH

*(To **Tybalt**)* Rise up, sir, and follow me. The prince demands
your obedience.

*(Enter the **prince**, along with the **Montagues** and **Capulets**)*

PRINCE

Who ignited this deadly clash?

BENVOLIO

O noble prince, I can discover all the unlucky manage of this fatal brawl: there lies the man, slain by young Romeo, that slew thy kinsman, brave Mercutio.

LADY CAPULET

Tybalt, my cousin! O my brother's child! O prince! O cousin! husband! O, the blood is spilt O my dear kinsman! Prince, as thou art true, For blood of ours, shed blood of Montague. O cousin, cousin!

PRINCE

Benvolio, who began this bloody fray?

BENVOLIO

Tybalt, here slain, whom Romeo's hand did slay; Romeo that spoke him fair, bade him bethink how nice the quarrel was, and urged withal your high displeasure: all this uttered with gentle breath, calm look, knees humbly bow'd, could not take truce with the unruly spleen of Tybalt deaf to peace, but that he tilts with piercing steel at bold Mercutio's breast, who all as hot, turns deadly point to point, and, with a martial scorn, with one hand beats cold death aside, and with the other sends it back to Tybalt, whose dexterity, retorts it: Romeo he cries aloud, 'hold, friends! friends, part!' and, swifter than his tongue, his agile arm beats down their fatal points, and 'twixt them rushes; underneath whose arm an envious thrust from Tybalt hit the life of stout Mercutio, and then Tybalt fled; but by and by comes back to Romeo, who had but newly entertain'd revenge, And to 't they go like lightning, for, ere I could draw to part them, was stout Tybalt slain. And, as

BENVOLIO

Your Highness, I'll tell you. Tybalt's there, cold. He dropped your
kin, good Mercutio, then Romeo dropped him.

LADY CAPULET

Tybalt, my kin! My brother's boy! Oh, Prince, my nephew's taken
from us! For honor's sake, you must balance this loss with a
Montague's blood. Oh, my cousin!

PRINCE

Benvolio, tell us who started this fight?

BENVOLIO

Tybalt who lies here, by Romeo's hand. Romeo tried to talk
sense, said the beef was weak, urged him to think of your
disapproval, to seek peace, all while speaking easy, calm, kneeling
even! But Tybalt's rage was deaf to any truce, and so, he lunged
with his blade at Mercutio's heart! Then after Tybalt bolted, he
came back, and Romeo, now with revenge on the brain, engaged.

he fell, did Romeo turn and fly. This is the truth, or let Benvolio die.

LADY CAPULET

He is a kinsman to the Montague; affection makes him false; he speaks not true: some twenty of them fought in this black strife, and all those twenty could but kill one life. I beg for justice, which thou, prince, must give; Romeo slew Tybalt, Romeo must not live.

PRINCE

Romeo slew him, he slew Mercutio; Who now the price of his dear blood doth owe?

MONTAGUE

Not Romeo, prince, he was Mercutio's friend; his fault concludes but what the law should end, the life of Tybalt.

PRINCE

And for that offence immediately we do exile him hence: I have an interest in your hate's proceeding, my blood for your rude brawls doth lie a-bleeding; but I'll amerce you with so strong a fine that you shall all repent the loss of mine: I will be deaf to pleading and excuses; nor tears nor prayers shall purchase out abuses: therefore use none: let Romeo hence in haste, else, when he's found, that hour is his last. bear hence this body and attend our will: mercy but murders, pardoning those that kill.

(Exeunt)

It was over in a flash—Tybalt fell, and Romeo took off. ISTG, that's how it went down!

LADY CAPULET

He's Montague's crew, that's super sus! He claims Tybalt caused this drama, but it took all of them to take down just one! Justice is what I seek, Prince! It was Romeo who clapped Tybalt's cheeks, and for that, he should get murked!

PRINCE

Romeo indeed deleted Tybalt, who had himself deleted Mercutio. Now, who should answer for Mercutio being deleted?

MONTAGUE

Prince, not Romeo. He was but avenging his friend Mercutio—Tybalt's death was the law's work, not his crime!

PRINCE

For his part, Romeo shall be banished from Verona! I've lost my bestie Mercutio, to your beef, and it's you, the fams, who'll feel the weight of my wrath! No apologies or retweets will change this! Romeo must dip from the city at once! If he's found, he is canceled! This is the price of violence—mercy would only breed more killing.

(And with that, they leave the scene)

ACT THREE

SCENE TWO

*(Enter **Juliet**)*

JULIET

Gallop apace, you fiery-footed steeds, towards Phoebus' lodging: such a wagoner as Phaethon would whip you to the west, and bring in cloudy night immediately. Spread thy close curtain, love-performing night, that runaway's eyes may wink and Romeo leap to these arms, untalk'd of and unseen. Lovers can see to do their amorous rites by their own beauties; or, if love be blind, it best agrees with night. Come, civil night, thou sober-suited matron, all in black, and learn me how to lose a winning match, play'd for a pair of stainless maidenhoods: hood my unmann'd blood, bating in my cheeks, with thy black mantle; till strange love, grown bold, think true love acted simple modesty. Come, night; come, Romeo; come, thou day in night; for thou wilt lie upon the wings of night whiter than new snow on a raven's back. Come, gentle night, come, loving, black-brow'd night, give me my Romeo; and, when he shall die, take him and cut him out in little stars, and he will make the face of heaven so fine that all the world will be in love with night and pay no worship to the garish sun. O, I have bought the mansion of a love, but not possess'd it, and, though I am sold, not yet enjoy'd: so tedious is this day as is the night before some festival to an impatient child that hath new robes and may not wear them. O, here comes my nurse, and she brings news; and every tongue that speaks but Romeo's name speaks heavenly eloquence.

*(Enter **nurse**, with cords)*

ACT THREE

SCENE TWO

*(Enter **Juliet** alone)*

JULIET

'Sun, could you not?' I need it to be night, like, now. When its dark out, Romeo shall slide through for some Netflix and chill, beauty has that night vision, to let lovers get down in the dark. I'm ready for night to come like an emo chick in all black, to let Romeo teach me a losing game where I bet my virginity. Let me not be cringe and figure out this game of love so that it is pure, modest, and on point. Roll up, night. Giv'eth me my Romeo, who shines brighter than snow on a raven's wing. Come at me, sweet night. Come at me, love. Bring'eth me my Romeo. And when I peace out, make him a constellation in the nigh sky, shining bright. His glow-up will make the universe so dope that everyone will Stan the night and unfollow the sun. Oh, I have bought the mansion of love, but not moved in, and though I am sold, I'm not yet enjoyed.

*(The **nurse** enters)*

Aye, here's my nurse, she brings forth the news. Every mention of Romeo's name is like a song that slaps. So, what's good, nurse? Tis that the rope ladder Romeo had you get?

NURSE

Ay, ay, the cords.

JULIET

Ay me! what news? why dost thou wring thy hands?

NURSE

Ah, well-a-day! he's dead, he's dead, he's dead! We are undone,
lady, we are undone! Alack the day! he's gone, he's kill'd, he's
dead!

JULIET

Can heaven be so envious?

NURSE

Romeo can, though heaven cannot: O Romeo, Romeo! Who ever
would have thought it? Romeo!

JULIET

What devil art thou, that dost torment me thus? This torture
should be roar'd in dismal hell. Hath Romeo slain himself? say
thou but 'I,' and that bare vowel 'I' shall poison more than the
death-darting eye of cockatrice: I am not I, if there be such an I;
or those eyes shut, that make thee answer 'I.' if he be slain, say 'I';
or if not, no: brief sounds determine of my weal or woe.

NURSE

Facts, facts, tis the rope ladder.

JULIET

Spill the tea, why thy face so long?

NURSE

He's dead. Ghosted! We're getting canceled girl, it's the worst!
He's out! Got clapped! Gone!

JULIET

Is it even fair for the universe to throw this much shade?

NURSE

Romeo is the one causing the drama! Oh, Romeo, who
would've thought it would be thee?

JULIET

You for real rn? What a troll you are to vibe check me so hard?
Hast Romeo unalived himself? Just hit me with a "yes" and that
one word could send me over the edge! I can't even, if you tell
me Romeo's done himself in. If he's been taken out, say "Yes." If
not, "Nay." These few words are like, my entire vibe!

NURSE

I saw the wound, I saw it with mine eyes,- God save the mark!--
here on his manly breast: a piteous corse, a bloody piteous corse;
pale, pale as ashes, all bedaub'd in blood, all in gore-blood; I
swounded at the sight.

JULIET

O, break, my heart! poor bankrupt, break at once! To prison,
eyes, ne'er look on liberty! Vile earth, to earth resign; end motion
here; and thou and Romeo press one heavy bier!

NURSE

O Tybalt, Tybalt, the best friend I had! O courteous Tybalt!
honest gentleman! That ever I should live to see thee dead!

JULIET

What storm is this that blows so contrary? Is Romeo slaughter'd,
and is Tybalt dead? My dear-loved cousin, and my dearer lord?
Then, dreadful trumpet, sound the general doom! For who is
living, if those two are gone?

NURSE

Tybalt is gone, and Romeo banished; Romeo that kill'd him, he is
banished.

JULIET

O God! did Romeo's hand shed Tybalt's blood?

NURSE

I saw it with my own eyes. That wound though, right there on his chiseled chest! A tragic scene, a bloody tragic scene! As pale as a ghost, soaked in blood! I was shook to the core, passed out cold!

JULIET

Oh snap! My heart! It's breaking! I lock away my eyes to never see again! I shall return my body to the earth! I'm done moving! Put me in the coffin with Romeo! RIP!

NURSE

Tybalt, my dude, you were A1, the realest! Oh, honorable Tybalt, you were a chill bro. O' that ever I should live to see thee dead.

JULIET

What is this mess? Romeo's been murked, and Tybalt too? Tybalt was fam, my day one! And Romeo, was my main squeeze! What's the point if those two are out of the game?

NURSE

Tybalt's been deleted, and Romeo's been banned. Romeo dropped Tybalt, and now he must dip out of town.

JULIET

Frfr? Romeo's hands did that to Tybalt?

NURSE

It did, it did; alas the day, it did!

JULIET

O serpent heart, hid with a flowering face! Did ever dragon keep
so fair a cave? Beautiful tyrant! fiend angelical! Dove-feather'd
raven! wolvish-ravening lamb! Despised substance of divinest
show! Just opposite to what thou justly seem'st, a damned saint, an
honourable villain! O nature, what hadst thou to do in hell, when
thou didst bower the spirit of a fiend in moral paradise of such
sweet flesh? Was ever book containing such vile matter so fairly
bound? O that deceit should dwell in such a gorgeous palace!

NURSE

There's no trust, no faith, no honesty in men; all perjured, all
forsworn, all naught, all dissemblers. Ah, where's my man? give
me some aqua vitae: these griefs, these woes, these sorrows make
me old. Shame come to Romeo!

JULIET

Blister'd be thy tongue for such a wish! he was not born to shame:
upon his brow shame is ashamed to sit; for 'tis a throne where
honour may be crown'd sole monarch of the universal earth. O,
what a beast was I to chide at him!

NURSE

Will you speak well of him that kill'd your cousin?

NURSE

Facts! Wish it wasn't so, but yeah, it happened.

JULIET

Bruh, he catfished me, that angel-faced devil! Did a dragon ever
lurk in such a beautiful cave? He's got the soft look of a dove but
plays the game like a wolf! I'm so over him, even though having
him was #Goals. He's flipped the script, totally not what he
posted. What a scam, he seemed so legit. Seriously, nature, what
kind of glitch was that? Crafting a demon's soul in a snack's body?
Was there ever such an evil book so fairly bound?

NURSE

No cap, there's zero chill, no loyalty, no realness in dudes. They're
all cap, all sliding into DMs. All of them are sus. Yo, where's my
servant? —I need a drink.—All this drama, these vibes are aging
me.

JULIET

I should report you for talking like that! He wasn't made to catch
all this shade! My man is a real one! He's all about the respect, full-
on honor. I'm lowkey wild for throwing him any shade!

NURSE

You gonna hype up the one who ended your fam?

JULIET

Shall I speak ill of him that is my husband? Ah, poor my lord, what tongue shall smooth thy name, when I, thy three-hours wife, have mangled it? But, wherefore, villain, didst thou kill my cousin? That villain cousin would have kill'd my husband: back, foolish tears, back to your native spring; your tributary drops belong to woe, which you, mistaking, offer up to joy. My husband lives, that Tybalt would have slain; and Tybalt's dead, that would have slain my husband: all this is comfort; wherefore weep I then? Some word there was, worser than Tybalt's death, that murder'd me: I would forget it fain; but, O, it presses to my memory, like damned guilty deeds to sinners' minds: 'Tybalt is dead, and Romeo--banished;' that 'banished,' that one word 'banished,' hath slain ten thousand Tybalts. Tybalt's death was woe enough, if it had ended there: or, if sour woe delights in fellowship and needly will be rank'd with other griefs, why follow'd not, when she said 'Tybalt's dead,' thy father, or thy mother, nay, or both, which modern lamentations might have moved? But with a rear-ward following Tybalt's death, 'Romeo is banished,' to speak that word, is father, mother, Tybalt, Romeo, Juliet, all slain, all dead. 'Romeo is banished!' There is no end, no limit, measure, bound, in that word's death; no words can that woe sound. Where is my father, and my mother, nurse?

NURSE

Weeping and wailing over Tybalt's corse: will you go to them? I will bring you thither.

JULIET

Am I really gonna throw shade at my own man? Sheesh, my
dude, who's gonna hype you up now, when your wifey of just a few
hours is straight up dragging you? But why, bro, why'd you have to
do my cousin like that? 'Cause he was coming for you, right? I
ain't crying, no tears here. I should be happy 'cause you're still
here, but still, I'm lowkey sad 'cause Tybalt's not. My man's alive,
and the one who wanted him gone is done. That's supposed to
feel good, right? So why am I crying? There's worse news than
Tybalt's death. News that's got me wanting to hit cancel on life
itself. "Tybalt's gone, and Romeo's cancelled. "That "cancelled" bit
is harsher than if a whole squad of Tybalts got murked. If it was
just "Tybalt's gone," maybe I could handle it. Pain's always looking
for a plus-one, huh? Would've been less of a drag if, after "Tybalt's
gone, she hit me with "your folks are gone too." That would've
been normal sad. But dropping "Tybalt's gone" and then "Romeo's
cancelled," is like saying everyone's gone—my fam, my Tybalt, my
Romeo, and me, we're all just... it's all over. "Romeo's cancelled."
That's like a black hole of RIPs. No emoji can show this kind of
hurt. Where are my parents at, nurse?

NURSE

They're over there, making a scene over Tybalt's body. You gonna
roll up with them? I'll take you over there.

JULIET

Wash they his wounds with tears: mine shall be spent, when theirs are dry, for Romeo's banishment. Take up those cords: poor ropes, you are beguiled, both you and I; for Romeo is exiled: he made you for a highway to my bed; but I, a maid, die maiden-widowed. Come, cords, come, nurse; I'll to my wedding-bed; and death, not Romeo, take my maidenhead!

NURSE

Hie to your chamber: I'll find Romeo to comfort you: I wot well where he is. Hark ye, your Romeo will be here at night: I'll to him; he is hid at Laurence' cell.

JULIET

O, find him! give this ring to my true knight, and bid him come to take his last farewell.

(Exeunt)

JULIET

They're out there hitting refresh with their tears, huh? I'll drop my own when their well's dry, all 'cause Romeo's gotta bounce. Grab this rope ladder. This thing's useless now, just like me, 'cause Romeo's banished. It was supposed to be a highway to my bed for him, but here I am, still on read, and gonna stay that way—a virgin and a widow. And it's gonna be the forever sleep that snatches my status, not Romeo.

NURSE

Skedaddle to your room. I'll fetch Romeo, I know his @. You and Romeo can Netflix and chill tonight. I'll go find him. He's laying low at Friar Laurence's spot.

JULIET

(Handing over a ring) Bet, find my main squeeze! Pass him this and tell him he needs to come through for the final scene.

(They exit)

ACT THREE

SCENE THREE

*(Enter **Friar Laurence**)*

FRIAR LAURENCE

Romeo, come forth; come forth, thou fearful man: affliction is
enamour'd of thy parts, and thou art wedded to calamity.

*(Enter **Romeo**)*

ROMEO

Father, what news? what is the prince's doom? What sorrow
craves acquaintance at my hand, that I yet know not?

FRIAR LAURENCE

Too familiar is my dear son with such sour company: I bring thee
tidings of the prince's doom.

ROMEO

What less than dooms-day is the prince's doom?

ACT THREE

SCENE THREE

(Friar Laurence enters)

FRIAR LAURENCE

Yo, Romeo, slide out; come hither, you shook one. Trouble has a thing for you, and you're basically married to it now.

(Romeo enters)

ROMEO

Yo, Father, what's the news? What's the prince's vibe? What kind of consequences am I facing? I'm still in the dark.

FRIAR LAURENCE

Bro, calm down. I got the scoop on the prince's decision.

ROMEO

Is the Prince's play any less harsh than judgment day?

FRIAR LAURENCE

A gentler judgment vanish'd from his lips, not body's death, but body's banishment.

ROMEO

Ha, banishment! be merciful, say 'death;' for exile hath more terror in his look, much more than death: do not say 'banishment.'

FRIAR LAURENCE

Hence from Verona art thou banished: be patient, for the world is broad and wide.

ROMEO

There is no world without Verona walls, but purgatory, torture, hell itself. Hence-banished is banish'd from the world, and world's exile is death: then banished, is death mis-term'd: calling death banishment, thou cutt'st my head off with a golden axe, and smilest upon the stroke that murders me.

FRIAR LAURENCE

O deadly sin! O rude unthankfulness! Thy fault our law calls death; but the kind prince, taking thy part, hath rush'd aside the law, and turn'd that black word death to banishment: this is dear mercy, and thou seest it not.

FRIAR LAURENCE

He went soft on you. You ain't gonna die, but you're getting banned from the city.

ROMEO

Aye, banned? Might as well just say "GG". Being banned is way harsher than death. Don't say "banned"!

FRIAR LAURENCE

From here on out, you're banned from Verona. You gotta roll with it fam, it's a big world out there.

ROMEO

Nah, there's no stage for me beyond Verona's gates, just big L's, torture, the shadow realm itself! Getting banned from Verona's like being banned from the whole world, and being banned from the world is just as bad as getting unalived. Saying the word "banned" instead of "death" is basically smiling in my face while you cut my head off with a golden axe.

FRIAR LAURENCE

Big oof! Oh, salty and ungrateful, dude! Our law says you're donezo, but the chill prince, taking your side, hit pause on the law, and switched the punishment from 'death' to 'you're blocked'. That's legit mercy, and you're sleeping on it.

ROMEO

'Tis torture, and not mercy: heaven is here, where Juliet lives; and
every cat and dog and little mouse, every unworthy thing, live here
in heaven and may look on her; but Romeo may not: more
validity, more honourable state, more courtship lives in carrion-
flies than Romeo: they my seize on the white wonder of dear
Juliet's hand And steal immortal blessing from her lips, who even
in pure and vestal modesty, still blush, as thinking their own kisses
sin; but Romeo may not; he is banished: flies may do this, but I
from this must fly: they are free men, but I am banished. And
say'st thou yet that exile is not death? Hadst thou no poison mix'd,
no sharp-ground knife, no sudden mean of death, though ne'er so
mean, but 'banished' to kill me?--'banished'? O friar, the damned
use that word in hell; howlings attend it: how hast thou the heart,
being a divine, a ghostly confessor, a sin-absolver, and my friend
profess'd, to mangle me with that word 'banished'?

FRIAR LAURENCE

Thou fond mad man, hear me but speak a word.

ROMEO

O, thou wilt speak again of banishment.

FRIAR LAURENCE

I'll give thee armour to keep off that word: adversity's sweet milk,
philosophy, to comfort thee, though thou art banished.

ROMEO

This is straight-up torture, not a mercy! 'Cause for real, heaven's got nothing on this place where Juliet's at. Every critter here, from cats and dogs to the smallest mouse, gets to peep at her, but Romeo's blacklisted. Flies get to live the high life, more noble and fit for love than I'll ever be. They get to touch Juliet's bomb white hand, score kisses on her lips, while she's all innocent and blushing, thinking even their bug smooches are too bold. And Romeo? I'm hit with the ban hammer, can't even hold her hand. These flies are out here free, living it up, and I'm slapped with an exile. And you're trying to say being banned isn't a death sentence? Didn't have anything quicker to end me, like poison or a sharp blade? Nothing but this disgrace of banishment? Yo, Friar, even the lost souls in the bad place scream about banishment. If you're supposed to be this holy dude who forgives sins and you claim you're my homie, how can you even lay that word on me without wincing?

FRIAR LAURENCE

You're wildin, fam! Just listen a sec!

ROMEO

What? Are we gonna talk about banishment some more?

FRIAR LAURENCE

I'll shield you from that word, I got you. Here's the real deal, the cure for your drama: philosophy. That's gonna come in clutch, even if you're out here banned.

ROMEO

Yet 'banished'? Hang up philosophy! Unless philosophy can make a Juliet, displant a town, reverse a prince's doom, it helps not, it prevails not: talk no more.

FRIAR LAURENCE

O, then I see that madmen have no ears.

ROMEO

How should they, when that wise men have no eyes?

FRIAR LAURENCE

Let me dispute with thee of thy estate.

ROMEO

Thou canst not speak of that thou dost not feel: wert thou as young as I, Juliet thy love, an hour but married, Tybalt murdered, doting like me and like me banished, then mightst thou speak, then mightst thou tear thy hair, and fall upon the ground, as I do now, taking the measure of an unmade grave.

(Knocking within)

FRIAR LAURENCE

Arise; one knocks; good Romeo, hide thyself.

ORIGINAL TEXT

ROMEO

There's that word again, "banned". Drop the philosophy, man!
Unless philosophy can spawn a Juliet, relocate a whole town, or
flip the prince's script, it's just talk. Save your breath!

FRIAR LAURENCE

Dang, so you're not even going to listen?

ROMEO

How's a madman gonna listen if the so-called wise are blind?

FRIAR LAURENCE

Chill, let me break it down for you.

ROMEO

You can't school me on feels you haven't felt. If you were as
young as me, and Juliet was your bae, and you just made her your
wifey, then you murked Tybalt, and you were as shook and
lovesick as I am, and got yeeted with a ban. Then you might get
where I'm coming from. Then you might lose your wig, falling to
the floor like I am right now. (*Romeo* drops to the ground)
You'd be the one kneeling, sizing up a spot for a dirt nap.

(*We hear knocking offstage*)

FRIAR LAURENCE

Yo, get up. There's someone at the door. Time to dip, Romeo.

ROMEO

Not I; unless the breath of heartsick groans, mist-like, infold me from the search of eyes.

(Knocking)

FRIAR LAURENCE

Hark, how they knock! Who's there? Romeo, arise; thou wilt be taken. Stay awhile! Stand up.

(Knocking)

Run to my study. By and by! God's will, what simpleness is this! I come, I come!

(Knocking)

Who knocks so hard? whence come you? what's your will?

NURSE

(Within) Let me come in, and you shall know my errand; I come from Lady Juliet.

FRIAR LAURENCE

Welcome, then.

*(Enter **nurse**)*

ROMEO

Nah, not me; maybe my sadboi vibes, like a fog, can shield me from those prying eyes.

(Knocking)

FRIAR LAURENCE

Yo, the knocking's not stopping! *—(To the person at the door)* Just a sec! *—(To **Romeo**)* Romeo, get up, bro. They'll bust you. *—(To the person at the door)* Chill for a sec.*—(To **Romeo**)* Get on your feet, man!

(Knocking)

Duck into my study—Just hang on—Why you gotta play the fool? *(To the person at the door)* Hang tight. I'm coming, I swear!

(Knocking)

Why you gotta bust down my door? What's your deal? Who is it?

NURSE

(From offstage) Yo, let me in, and I'll spill why I'm here. Lady Juliet sent me!

FRIAR LAURENCE

(To the person at the door) Alright then, come through.

*(The **nurse** comes in)*

NURSE

O holy friar, O, tell me, holy friar, where is my lady's lord, where's Romeo?

FRIAR LAURENCE

There on the ground, with his own tears made drunk.

NURSE

O, he is even in my mistress' case, just in her case! O woful sympathy! Piteous predicament! Even so lies she, blubbering and weeping, weeping and blubbering. Stand up, stand up; stand, and you be a man: for Juliet's sake, for her sake, rise and stand; why should you fall into so deep an O?

ROMEO

Nurse!

NURSE

Ah sir! ah sir! Well, death's the end of all.

ROMEO

Spakest thou of Juliet? how is it with her?Doth she not think me an old murderer, now I have stain'd the childhood of our joy with blood removed but little from her own? Where is she? And how doth she? and what says my conceal'd lady to our cancell'd love?

NURSE

Oh, holy man, give it to me straight, where's my girl's main squeeze? Where's Romeo at?

FRIAR LAURENCE

Look there, dude's down on the floor, drunk on tears.

NURSE

Oh snap, he's just like Juliet, same thing different font. Man, the feels are hitting different! She's got the same drama, on the floor, crying a river, just like him, sobbing her heart out. Stand the heck up! Get up, if you're a man! For Juliet's sake, get up! Why you gotta be doing so much?

ROMEO

Nurse!

NURSE

Hey sir, hey. Death's the finale for us all, ain't it?

ROMEO

You talking 'bout Juliet? What's the vibe with her? Does she think I'm a stone-cold killer now 'cause I dirtied our fresh start by icing her cuz? Where she at? How's she holding up? What's my babygirl saying 'bout our canceled love story?

NURSE

O, she says nothing, sir, but weeps and weeps; and now falls on her bed; and then starts up, and Tybalt calls; and then on Romeo cries, and then down falls again.

ROMEO

As if that name, shot from the deadly level of a gun, did murder her; as that name's cursed hand murder'd her kinsman. O, tell me, friar, tell me, in what vile part of this anatomy doth my name lodge? tell me, that I may sack the hateful mansion. *(Drawing his sword)*

FRIAR LAURENCE

Hold thy desperate hand: art thou a man? thy form cries out thou art: thy tears are womanish; thy wild acts denote the unreasonable fury of a beast: unseemly woman in a seeming man! Or ill-beseeming beast in seeming both! Thou hast amazed me: by my holy order, I thought thy disposition better temper'd. Hast thou slain Tybalt? wilt thou slay thyself? And stay thy lady too that lives in thee, by doing damned hate upon thyself? Why rail'st thou on thy birth, the heaven, and earth? Since birth, and heaven, and earth, all three do meet in thee at once; which thou at once wouldst lose. Fie, fie, thou shamest thy shape, thy love, thy wit; which, like a usurer, abound'st in all, and usest none in that true use indeed which should bedeck thy shape, thy love, thy wit: thy noble shape is but a form of wax, digressing from the valour of a man; thy dear love sworn but hollow perjury, killing that love which thou hast vow'd to cherish; thy wit, that ornament to shape and love, misshapen in the conduct of them both, like powder in a skitless soldier's flask, is set afire by thine own ignorance, and thou dismember'd with thine own defence. What, rouse thee, man! thy Juliet is alive, for whose dear sake thou wast but lately dead; there art thou happy: Tybalt would kill thee, but thou slew'st Tybalt;

NURSE

Nah, she straight-up isn't sayin much bro. Just crying a river, yeets onto her bed, then trying to rise up. Calls out for Tybalt, then for you, and down she goes again.

ROMEO

It's like my name's a bullet, killing her like I offed her cuz. Yo, Friar, where's my name hiding in me? Point it out, so I can cut it out! *(He whips out his dagger)*

FRIAR LAURENCE

Cool it, don't go off the deep end! You're a man, right? You look the part, but you're crying like a girl! Your wild actions are giving... wild animal, no cap. You're like a zesty woman dressed as a man, or some twisted creature, half dude, half beast! You've got me shook, I swear on my holy order, I thought you had more brains, and more chill than this. Did you drop Tybalt? Gonna drop yourself next? And end the girl who's living through you? Why are you throwing hands with your own existence, bruh? Life's like the VIP pass, but you're about to yeet it all! You're shaming your own self, your heart, your mind. You got all these gifts, but you're hoarding them like a boomer with cash, not using them where they count—your body, your love, your thoughts. Your body's just a prop, without the honor of a man. Your love's like a bad joke. You're killing the very love you swore was so bussin. Your brain, meant to guide your heart and your actions, you trolled them both. You're like a rookie soldier who blows himself up 'cause he's careless. The tools you got for protection you're using with an uno reverse. Rise up, bro! Your Juliet's still in the chat! It was for her you nearly got clapped. Be glad she's still here! Tybalt was out for your head, but you got him first. Be thankful you're here! The law

there are thou happy too: the law that threaten'd death becomes
thy friend and turns it to exile; there art thou happy: a pack of
blessings lights up upon thy back; happiness courts thee in her
best array; but, like a misbehaved and sullen wench, thou pout'st
upon thy fortune and thy love: take heed, take heed, for such die
miserable. Go, get thee to thy love, as was decreed, ascend her
chamber, hence and comfort her: but look thou stay not till the
watch be set, for then thou canst not pass to Mantua; where thou
shalt live, till we can find a time to blaze your marriage, reconcile
your friends, beg pardon of the prince, and call thee back with
twenty hundred thousand times more joy than thou went'st forth
in lamentation. Go before, nurse: commend me to thy lady; and
bid her hasten all the house to bed, which heavy sorrow makes
them apt unto: Romeo is coming.

NURSE

O Lord, I could have stay'd here all the night to hear good
counsel: O, what learning is! My lord, I'll tell my lady you will
come.

ROMEO

Do so, and bid my sweet prepare to chide.

NURSE

Here, sir, a ring she bid me give you, sir: hie you, make haste, for
it grows very late. *(Exit **nurse**)*

ROMEO

How well my comfort is revived by this!

had you marked, but now it's just a timeout. Find the good in that. Your life's still full of W's. But you, acting all zesty and outta pocket, complaining about your life and your love. Listen, those who vibe like that, they don't end well. Roll out to your girl, like you promised when you cuffed her up. Get to her room, give her some peace. But make sure to bounce before the guards come through. Then head to Mantua, hang there until we can blast your wedding news, fix the beef with your fams. We'll @ the Prince to slide you a pardon. Then you can return to the chat with more hype than the drama you're leaving with. Scoot, Nurse. Pass my words to your girl, tell her to hustle everyone to bed. They must be wrecked with sadness. Romeo's about to pull up!

NURSE

For real, I could kick it here all-night soaking in that boomer wisdom. Smart dude! *(To **Romeo**)* Aight, my lord, I'll spill the tea to your bae.

ROMEO

Bet, tell her she is free to roast me.

NURSE

Oh, BTW, she sent me to drop this ring off for you. Step on it, it's getting mad late. *(Hands over **Juliet's** ring)*

*(The **nurse** heads out)*

ROMEO

Lesgoo!

FRIAR LAURENCE

Go hence; good night; and here stands all your state: either be gone before the watch be set, or by the break of day disguised from hence: Sojourn in Mantua; I'll find out your man, and he shall signify from time to time every good hap to you that chances here: give me thy hand; 'tis late: farewell; good night.

ROMEO

But that a joy past joy calls out on me, it were a grief, so brief to part with thee: Farewell.

(Exeunt)

FRIAR LAURENCE

A'ight, time to roll. Peace out. Everything is riding on you getting out safe so dip out before the night crew comes through or ninja your way out at dawn. Crash in Mantua; I'll hunt down your boy, he'll keep you posted with all the news: slap me some skin, catch ya later, good night.

ROMEO

This quick goodbye is low-key sad but mad happiness is calling my name.

(They split)

ACT THREE

SCENE FOUR

*(Enter **Capulet**, **Lady Capulet**, and **Paris**)*

CAPULET

Things have fall'n out, sir, so unluckily, that we have had no time to move our daughter: look you, she loved her kinsman Tybalt dearly, and so did I:--well, we were born to die. 'Tis very late, she'll not come down to-night: I promise you, but for your company, I would have been a-bed an hour ago.

PARIS

These times of woe afford no time to woo. Madam, good night: commend me to your daughter.

LADY CAPULET

I will, and know her mind early to-morrow; to-night she is mew'd up to her heaviness.

ACT THREE

SCENE FOUR

*(Enter **Capulet**, **Lady Capulet**, and **Paris**)*

CAPULET

Yo, life's been straight-up messy, dude, no cap. We haven't slid our daughter the update on tying the knot with you yet. Listen, she was down for her cuz Tybalt, for real, and me too. But yo, we all gotta die sometime. It's hella late, she ain't gonna make an appearance tonight. Frfr, if you weren't chilling here, I'd be catching Zs already.

PARIS

In these dark times, ain't nobody got time for love! Lady C, nighty night: slide a 'what's good' to my bae for me.

LADY CAPULET

Got you. I'mma scope out her headspace on this whole wedding biz first thing. Tonight, she's locked up in her feels.

CAPULET

Sir Paris, I will make a desperate tender of my child's love: I think
she will be ruled in all respects by me; nay, more, I doubt it not.
Wife, go you to her ere you go to bed; acquaint her here of my
son Paris' love; and bid her, mark you me, on Wednesday next--
but, soft! what day is this?

PARIS

Monday, my lord,

CAPULET

Monday! ha, ha! Well, Wednesday is too soon, O' Thursday let it
be: o' Thursday, tell her, she shall be married to this noble earl.
Will you be ready? do you like this haste? We'll keep no great
ado,--a friend or two; for, hark you, Tybalt being slain so late, it
may be thought we held him carelessly, being our kinsman, if we
revel much: therefore we'll have some half a dozen friends, and
there an end. But what say you to Thursday?

PARIS

My lord, I would that Thursday were to-morrow.

CAPULET

Well get you gone: o' Thursday be it, then. Go you to Juliet ere
you go to bed, prepare her, wife, against this wedding-day.
Farewell, my lord. Light to my chamber, ho! Afore me! it is so
very very late, that we may call it early by and by. Good night.

(Exeunt)

CAPULET

A'ight, Sir Paris, let's talk about the love between you and my daughter. I'm thinking she'll vibe with it cuz, she listens to me, no doubt fam. Yo, wifey, make a pit stop in her chamber before you hit the sack. Hype her for my boy Paris'. And yo, listen up, next Wednesday- holdup what's the day today?

PARIS

It's Monday, fam.

CAPULET

Monday! Ha, ha! A'ight, Wednesday's mad rushed. Let's shoot for Thursday. Real talk, tell her, she's gonna be wifey to this legit earl. You cool with that? You think we're rushing it too fast? No need to throw a banger—we can roll with just the homies. With Tybalt just recently getting clapped and all, folks might say we don't give a flip. So, we'll keep it chill, just a small crew at the wedding. How you vibing with Thursday?

PARIS

Dude, I'm wishing Thursday was like, right now!

CAPULET

Bet. Bounce back to your crib. Thursday it is then. *(To **Lady Capulet**)* Go check in on Juliet before you bounce to bed. Prep her for the big day. *(To **Paris**)* Later, dude. I'm out to catch some Z's! Dang, it's so late it's practically morning; good night.

(Exit)

ACT THREE

SCENE FIVE

*(Enter **Romeo** and **Juliet** above, at the window)*

JULIET

Wilt thou be gone? it is not yet near day: it was the nightingale, and not the lark, that pierced the fearful hollow of thine ear; nightly she sings on yon pomegranate-tree: believe me, love, it was the nightingale.

ROMEO

It was the lark, the herald of the morn, no nightingale: look, love, what envious streaks do lace the severing clouds in yonder east: night's candles are burnt out, and jocund day stands tiptoe on the misty mountain tops. I must be gone and live, or stay and die.

JULIET

Yon light is not day-light, I know it, I: it is some meteor that the sun exhales, to be to thee this night a torch-bearer, and light thee on thy way to Mantua: therefore stay yet; thou need'st not to be gone.

ACT THREE

SCENE FIVE

*(**Romeo** and **Juliet** enter above the stage)*

JULIET

Are you dipping? Chill, it ain't near sunrise. Fear not that tune, on God it's the nightingale, not the lark. Each eve the nightingale spits some bars in the pomegranate-tree. Trust, bae, 'twas the nightingale.

ROMEO

Nah, 'twas the lark spitting bars, hyping up the dawn, not the nightingale. Look, bae, see those flecks of sunlight yeeting through the clouds yonder? The night's over, and day's about to come through. If I wanna live, I gotta bounce, if I stay, F's in the chat for me.

JULIET

That light is not daylight, I know it, fam. The sun yeeted a meteor to guide you to Mantua. Hang for a sec, you ain't gotta ghost just yet.

ROMEO

Let me be ta'en, let me be put to death; I am content, so thou wilt
have it so. I'll say yon grey is not the morning's eye, 'tis but the pale
reflex of Cynthia's brow; nor that is not the lark, whose notes do
beat the vaulty heaven so high above our heads: I have more care
to stay than will to go: come, death, and welcome! Juliet wills it so.
How is't, my soul? let's talk; it is not day.

JULIET

It is, it is: hie hence, be gone, away! It is the lark that sings so out
of tune, straining harsh discords and unpleasing sharps. Some say
the lark makes sweet division; this doth not so, for she divideth us:
some say the lark and loathed toad change eyes, O, now I would
they had changed voices too! Since arm from arm that voice doth
us affray, hunting thee hence with hunt's-up to the day, O, now be
gone; more light and light it grows.

ROMEO

More light and light; more dark and dark our woes!

*(Enter **nurse**)*

NURSE

Madam!

JULIET

Nurse?

ROMEO

Bet, take me in, let the world cancel me, I'm down, if that's your vibe, I'll say the glow's just a sick moon filter if you want. I'll cap and say that sound ain't the lark calling up the sun. I'm down to stay more than I wanna dip. Let's welcome the big sleep! Juliet's feeling it. So what's good my one and only? Wanna Netflix and chill some more? Tis no sunlight yet.

JULIET

Okay frfr, it is. Bounce now, make tracks. It's that lark spitting bars so off-key, bringing up the sun. Some say the lark splits the difference between nights and days. That's cap 'cause it's separating us. Some say the lark traded eyes with a toad. Bruh, I wish they swapped voices too! 'Cause now the lark's chirp is vibe checking us out of our feels, and soon the squad will be out here hunting for you. Slide out now, I see it's getting brighter and brighter.

ROMEO

Facts, more light means more trouble for us both.

*(The **nurse** enters)*

NURSE

Yo, Madam!

JULIET

What's good, nurse?

NURSE

Your lady mother is coming to your chamber: the day is broke; be wary, look about.

(Exit)

JULIET

Then, window, let day in, and let life out.

ROMEO

Farewell, farewell! one kiss, and I'll descend.

*(They kiss, **Romeo** descends)*

JULIET

Art thou gone so? love, lord, ay, husband, friend! I must hear from thee every day in the hour, for in a minute there are many days: O, by this count I shall be much in years ere I again behold my Romeo!

ROMEO

Farewell! I will omit no opportunity that may convey my greetings, love, to thee.

JULIET

O think'st thou we shall ever meet again?

NURSE

Your mom's pulling up to your room. It's a new day, wake up.
Stay sharp.

*(The **nurse** exits)*

JULIET

Alright window, bring in the day, send out my bae.

ROMEO

Deuces! Hit me with one last smooch, then I'm out.

*(They kiss and **Romeo** yeets the rope ladder)*

JULIET

Just like that, you're gone my bae? My main squeeze, my BFF!
You gotta slide into my DMs every hour on the hour. Every
minute's gonna feel like a decade. Bruh, I'll be ancient before I
get to see my Romeo again!

ROMEO

Bet, farewell! I'll slide into your DMs with my love!

JULIET

But frfr, you think we're gonna link up again?

ROMEO

I doubt it not; and all these woes shall serve for sweet discourses in our time to come.

JULIET

O God, I have an ill-divining soul! Methinks I see thee, now thou art below, as one dead in the bottom of a tomb: either my eyesight fails, or thou look'st pale.

ROMEO

And trust me, love, in my eye so do you: dry sorrow drinks our blood. Adieu, adieu!

(Exit)

JULIET

O fortune, fortune! all men call thee fickle: if thou art fickle, what dost thou with him. That is renown'd for faith? Be fickle, fortune; for then, I hope, thou wilt not keep him long, but send him back.

LADY CAPULET

(Within) Ho, daughter! are you up?

JULIET

Who is't that calls? is it my lady mother? Is she not down so late, or up so early? What unaccustom'd cause procures her hither?

ROMEO

No cap, and we'll turn all these L's into dope stories for the future.

JULIET

OMG, my vibes are so dark right now! I feel like I see you now, down there, looking like someone in a grave, either I'm going blind, or you're looking hella pale.

ROMEO

Trust, bae, you're looking kinda washed yourself: grief's sucking us dry. Later!

(*Romeo* has left the chat)

JULIET

Ugh, fortune, you're so extra. Everyone's like, "Fortune, make up your mind." Quit flip-floping so much, what's the plan for my ride-or-die Romeo? Get it together, fortune. Maybe you'll snap and send him back to me.

LADY CAPULET

(*Offstage*) Yo, Juliet! You up?

JULIET

Who dis? Mom? She's doing the most staying up this late. Or is it early? What's her deal even?

*(Enter **Lady Capulet**)*

LADY CAPULET

Why, how now, Juliet!

JULIET

Madam, I am not well.

LADY CAPULET

Evermore weeping for your cousin's death? What, wilt thou wash him from his grave with tears? An if thou couldst, thou couldst not make him live; therefore, have done: some grief shows much of love; but much of grief shows still some want of wit.

JULIET

Yet let me weep for such a feeling loss.

LADY CAPULET

So shall you feel the loss, but not the friend which you weep for.

JULIET

Feeling so the loss, cannot choose but ever weep the friend.

*(**Lady Capulet** enters the chat)*

LADY CAPULET

What's good, Juliet?

JULIET

Sis, I'm low-key feeling wrecked.

LADY CAPULET

You gonna be salty about Tybalt's logout forever? You think all these tears gonna bring him back? If tears were likes, it still wouldn't bring him back to your feed. Get a grip! A bit of sadness shows love, but you're looking like a major drama queen right now!

JULIET

Let me be in my feels, for this is a real loss.

LADY CAPULET

Feel the loss, sure, but the dude you weep for won't feel squat.

JULIET

I'm straight-up shook, can't just stop the feels.

LADY CAPULET

Well, girl, thou weep'st not so much for his death, as that the villain lives which slaughter'd him.

JULIET

What villain madam?

LADY CAPULET

That same villain, Romeo.

JULIET

(Aside) Villain and he be many miles asunder. God Pardon him! I do, with all my heart; and yet no man like he doth grieve my heart.

LADY CAPULET

That is, because the traitor murderer lives.

JULIET

Ay, madam, from the reach of these my hands: would none but I might venge my cousin's death!

LADY CAPULET

You're low-key crying not for the loss, but 'cause the jerk who did it is still out there.

JULIET

What jerk, madam?

LADY CAPULET

That jerk, Romeo!

JULIET

(Under her breath) He ain't no jerk. *(To **Lady Capulet**)* Bless him, for real. My heart's been hit hard, no one else can even.

LADY CAPULET

That's 'cause the backstabber is still alive.

JULIET

Yeah, 'cause he's outta my reach. Wish I could be the only one to clap back for Tybalt!

LADY CAPULET

We will have vengeance for it, fear thou not: then weep no more. I'll send to one in Mantua, where that same banish'd runagate doth live, shall give him such an unaccustom'd dram, that he shall soon keep Tybalt company: and then, I hope, thou wilt be satisfied.

JULIET

Indeed, I never shall be satisfied with Romeo, till I behold him-- dead-- Is my poor heart for a kinsman vex'd. Madam, if you could find out but a man to bear a poison, I would temper it; that Romeo should, upon receipt thereof, soon sleep in quiet. O, how my heart abhors to hear him named, and cannot come to him. To wreak the love I bore my cousin upon his body that slaughter'd him!

LADY CAPULET

Find thou the means, and I'll find such a man. But now I'll tell thee joyful tidings, girl.

JULIET

And joy comes well in such a needy time: what are they, I beseech your ladyship?

LADY CAPULET

Well, well, thou hast a careful father, child; one who, to put thee from thy heaviness, hath sorted out a sudden day of joy, that thou expect'st not nor I look'd not for.

LADY CAPULET

Bet, we're gonna clap back. Dry your eyes. I'll slide into Mantua, got a guy who'll serve Romeo a special cocktail, and he'll be chilling with Tybalt soon enough.

JULIET

Won't be cool with Romeo until I see him... Dead is how my heart feels when I think about my cuz. Find me someone to serve up that mix, I'll stir it myself, so he gets a quiet night. Can't stand people @ing him and I can't even go after him myself. I wanna channel all my love for my cuz and take it out on the body of Romeo.

LADY CAPULET

We'll find a way, and I'll find our guy. But check this, got some lit news for you.

JULIET

Hyped to get any good vibes right now. Spill it!

LADY CAPULET

So, your pops has been on the grind, he's planned a hype day to cancel your sadness. A day you weren't expecting.

JULIET

Madam, in happy time, what day is that?

LADY CAPULET

Marry, my child, early next Thursday morn, the gallant, young and noble gentleman, the County Paris, at Saint Peter's Church, shall happily make thee there a joyful bride.

JULIET

Now, by Saint Peter's Church and Peter too, he shall not make me there a joyful bride. I wonder at this haste; that I must wed ere he, that should be husband, comes to woo. I pray you, tell my lord and father, madam, I will not marry yet; and, when I do, I swear, it shall be Romeo, whom you know I hate, rather than Paris. These are news indeed!

LADY CAPULET

Here comes your father; tell him so yourself, and see how he will take it at your hands.

*(Enter **Capulet** and **nurse**)*

CAPULET

When the sun sets, the air doth drizzle dew; but for the sunset of my brother's son it rains downright. How now! a conduit, girl? what, still in tears? Evermore showering? In one little body thou counterfeit'st a bark, a sea, a wind; for still thy eyes, which I may call the sea, do ebb and flow with tears; the bark thy body is,

JULIET

Yo, hit me up with the deets, what's the day?

LADY CAPULET

Bet, at Saint Peter's Church when Thursday morning's rolls
around, the young, and fine Count Paris is gonna slide you a ring
and light up your world as your hubby.

JULIET

By Saint Peter's Church and the man, himself. He ain't gonna see
me all hyped up as a bride! This is all rushing at me; gotta pump
the brakes. How can I say "I do" to this dude without him even
sliding in my DMs first? Do me a solid. Tell my pops, your lord
and hubby, I ain't down for this! And if I ever change my status,
it's gonna be for Romeo—the one you think I throw shade at,
rather than Paris! No cap!

LADY CAPULET

Here's your dad. Drop this bombshell on him and see how he
vibes with it!

(Capulet and the nurse pull up)

CAPULET

Yo, when the sun dips, we get that drizzle. But ever since we lost
your cuz, it's like you're a walking rainstorm. What's good, Juliet?
You a fountain or something? You gonna cry it out forever? You
got all this drama in one little body—you're the ship, the sea, and

sailing in this salt flood; the winds, thy sighs; who, raging with thy
tears, and they with them, without a sudden calm, will overset thy
tempest-tossed body. How now, wife! Have you deliver'd to her
our decree?

LADY CAPULET

Ay, sir; but she will none, she gives you thanks. I would the fool
were married to her grave!

CAPULET

Soft! take me with you, take me with you, wife. How! will she
none? doth she not give us thanks? Is she not proud? doth she
not count her blest, unworthy as she is, that we have wrought so
worthy a gentleman to be her bridegroom?

JULIET

Not proud, you have; but thankful, that you have: proud can I
never be of what I hate; but thankful even for hate, that is meant
love.

CAPULET

How now, how now, chop-logic! What is this? 'Proud,' and 'I
thank you,' and 'I thank you not;' and yet 'not proud,' mistress
minion, you, thank me no thankings, nor, proud me no prouds,
but fettle your fine joints 'gainst Thursday next, to go with Paris to
Saint Peter's Church, or I will drag thee on a hurdle thither. Out,
you green-sickness carrion! out, you baggage! You tallow-face!

the storm all at once. Your eyes are like the ocean, just spilling tears. Your body's the ship, trying to sail through this salty flood. And your sighs are the wild winds. Girl, if you don't simmer down, this flood of feels is gonna drown you! Wifey, did you drop our news on her?

LADY CAPULET

Yeah, I did, but she's throwing major shade! She's all "thanks but no thanks," wishing she was in the dirt instead of heading down the aisle.

CAPULET

Hold up! What's this nonsense? She's saying no? She ain't thankful? Ain't feeling honored? She doesn't get how lit this match is? Can't she see she ain't even on his level?

JULIET

I ain't with what you're serving up, but I'm thankful you're serving something. I can't Stan what I hate, but props for the thought if it's coming from a place of love, you feel?

CAPULET

What kind of clownery is this? You're all "I'm thankful" and "thanks," then flipping to "nay" and "I ain't with it," acting all spoiled. You ain't showing any real gratitude or respect! But get your fit ready for Thursday! You're heading to Saint Peter's to get hitched to Paris! And if you ain't walking, I'm dragging you! You disgust me, you little twerp! You've lost it!

LADY CAPULET

Fie, fie! what, are you mad?

JULIET

Good father, I beseech you on my knees, hear me with patience but to speak a word.

CAPULET

Hang thee, young baggage! disobedient wretch! I tell thee what: get thee to church o' Thursday, or never after look me in the face: speak not, reply not, do not answer me; my fingers itch. Wife, we scarce thought us blest that God had lent us but this only child; but now I see this one is one too much, and that we have a curse in having her: out on her, hilding!

NURSE

God in heaven bless her! You are to blame, my lord, to rate her so.

CAPULET

And why, my lady wisdom? hold your tongue, good prudence; smatter with your gossips, go.

NURSE

I speak no treason.

LADY CAPULET

Chill, bro! You wildin'!

JULIET

Dad, please, I'm begging you, just listen to me for one sec!

CAPULET

Nah, I'm done with you, you little brat! You either show up at church on Thursday or never look at me again! Deadass, don't @ me, Don't DM me! I'll block you! *(Juliet stands up)* I'm so close to snapping! Wife, we never felt blessed having just one kid. But now I'm feeling one was too many! We got played the day she was born! She's straight-up cancelled in my eyes, that tramp!

NURSE

Oh bless her lord! She needs it! Sir, you're outta pocket roasting her like that!

CAPULET

You got something to say? Zip it, you old hag! Go run your mouth to your own subscribers!

NURSE

Im just keeping it a hundred.

CAPULET

O, God ye god-den.

NURSE

May not one speak?

CAPULET

Peace, you mumbling fool! Utter your gravity o'er a gossip's bowl;
for here we need it not.

LADY CAPULET

You are too hot.

CAPULET

God's bread! it makes me mad: day, night, hour, tide, time, work,
play, alone, in company, still my care hath been to have her
match'd: and having now provided a gentleman of noble
parentage, of fair demesnes, youthful, and nobly train'd, stuff'd, as
they say, with honourable parts, proportion'd as one's thought
would wish a man; and then to have a wretched puling fool, a
whining mammet, in her fortune's tender, to answer 'I'll not wed; I
cannot love, I am too young; I pray you, pardon me.' but, as you
will not wed, I'll pardon you: graze where you will you shall not
house with me: look to't, think on't, I do not use to jest. Thursday
is near; lay hand on heart, advise: an you be mine, I'll give you to
my friend; and you be not, hang, beg, starve, die in the streets, for,
by my soul, I'll ne'er acknowledge thee, nor what is mine shall
never do thee good: trust to't, bethink you; I'll not be forsworn.

CAPULET

Ugh, you're killing me!

NURSE

Am I not allowed to talk?

CAPULET

Put a sock in it, you troll! Keep your hot takes for your squad's group chat. This ain't the place.

LADY CAPULET

Oh, you're big mad!

CAPULET

It's got me heated because I have been going hard like all the time, like 24/7 no cap. I've been grinding to cop her a valid hubby. And now, I've bagged a chill bro from a family with clout, young, fresh, educated, the whole package! Any baddies dream! But this sad gurl, acting all emo, looks at this jackpot and is like, "Nah, this ain't it. Can't catch feels, too young, sorry not sorry." Bet, stay single then! You're free to ghost, but you ain't squatting under my roof! Frfr. Think on that! I ain't playing! It's going down on Thursday! If you're gonna rep this family, you'll say 'I do' to my guy. But if you act like a stranger, you can go kick rocks, beg, and drop dead for all I care! On God, if you're out then you're out! No cap!

(Capulet dips)

JULIET

Is there no pity sitting in the clouds, that sees into the bottom of my grief? O, sweet my mother, cast me not away! Delay this marriage for a month, a week; or, if you do not, make the bridal bed in that dim monument where Tybalt lies.

LADY CAPULET

Talk not to me, for I'll not speak a word: do as thou wilt, for I have done with thee.

(Exit)

JULIET

O God!--O nurse, how shall this be prevented? My husband is on earth, my faith in heaven; how shall that faith return again to earth, unless that husband send it me from heaven by leaving earth? comfort me, counsel me. Alack, alack, that heaven should practise stratagems upon so soft a subject as myself! What say'st thou? hast thou not a word of joy? Some comfort, nurse.

NURSE

Faith, here it is. Romeo is banish'd; and all the world to nothing, that he dares ne'er come back to challenge you; or, if he do, it needs must be by stealth. Then, since the case so stands as now it doth, I think it best you married with the county. O, he's a lovely gentleman! Romeo's a dishclout to him: an eagle, madam, hath not so green, so quick, so fair an eye as Paris hath. Beshrew my very heart, I think you are happy in this second match, for it excels your first: or if it did not, your first is dead; or 'twere as good he were, as living here and you no use of him.

JULIET

Is there no chill up in the heavens, that can see into my soul-deep grief? Moms, don't ghost me! Put the brakes on this thing for a month, a week, or if not, at least put my wedding bed down in the crypt where Tybalt's chilling!

LADY CAPULET

I'm muting this convo, do whatever. I'm out of your drama loop.

*(**Lady Capulet** has left the chat)*

JULIET

OMG—nurse, what's the plan? How do we stop this? My bae is still on Earth, but our wedding vows are locked in Heaven. How can I slide those vows back down unless Romeo hits up Heaven first to send them down? Hit me with some comfort, drop some advice. It's lame, the universe is playing games with a softie like me! You got anything? Like, any good vibes? Throw me a lifeline, nurse!

NURSE

Here it is. Romeo's out, like blocked for good. Not coming back. If he tries to slide back, he's gonna have to be like a ninja. So, look, that situation's messy, but the next move? Lock it down with the Count. Dude's a total catch, a snack! Compared to him, Romeo's basic, no cap. An eagle's got nothing on Paris's fair green eyes. It's a whole mood for your heart, and real talk, this second wedding might just be the glow-up you need, better than the OG one. Or if it's not, who cares? Romeo's MIA, you can't double-tap that anyway!

JULIET

Speakest thou from thy heart?

NURSE

And from my soul too; or else beshrew them both.

JULIET

Amen!

NURSE

What?

JULIET

Well, thou hast comforted me marvellous much. Go in: and tell
my lady I am gone, having displeased my father, to Laurence' cell,
to make confession and to be absolved.

NURSE

Marry, I will; and this is wisely done.

(Exit)

JULIET

Is that straight from the soul?

NURSE

Straight from the soul, frfr. Cross my heart, hope to die.

JULIET

Big mood!

NURSE

Huh?

JULIET

Cool story, Nurse. Now go tell my mom I've peaced out. Dads got me heated, so I'm off to Friar Laurence's to spill my guts and get that holy "it's all good".

NURSE

Bet, that's a solid plan.

*(The **nurse** heads out)*

JULIET

Ancient damnation! O most wicked fiend! Is it more sin to wish
me thus forsworn, or to dispraise my lord with that same tongue
which she hath praised him with above compare so many
thousand times? Go, counsellor; thou and my bosom henceforth
shall be twain. I'll to the friar, to know his remedy: if all else fail,
myself have power to die.

(Exit)

JULIET

This absolute Karen! What a snake, is it worse to want me to
break my word, or to trash my man with the same mouth you've
used to hype him to the heavens like a gazillion times? Bye,
Felicia! No more heart-to-hearts with you! I'm hitting up the friar
to cop his master plan. And if all else fails, I've still got one move
left – I can always cancel my own account!

(*Juliet* *leaves to hit up the Friar*)

ACT FOUR

SCENE ONE

*(Enter **Friar Laurence** and **Paris**)*

FRIAR LAURENCE

On Thursday, sir? the time is very short.

PARIS

My father Capulet will have it so; and I am nothing slow to slack
his haste.

FRIAR LAURENCE

You say you do not know the lady's mind: uneven is the course, I
like it not.

PARIS

Immoderately she weeps for Tybalt's death, and therefore have I
little talk'd of love; for Venus smiles not in a house of tears. Now,
sir, her father counts it dangerous that she doth give her sorrow so
much sway, and in his wisdom hastes our marriage, to stop the
inundation of her tears; which, too much minded by herself alone,
may be put from her by society: now do you know the reason of
this haste.

ACT FOUR

SCENE ONE

*(Enter **Friar Laurence** and **Paris**)*

FRIAR LAURENCE

On Thursday, fam? 'Tis, super soon.

PARIS

'Tis what Lord Capulet's pushing, and I'm here for it, no cap!

FRIAR LAURENCE

But, low-key you dont even know if the girl is feeling you? Thats tough, I'm not vibing with this at all.

PARIS

She's still big sad about Tybalt, RIP. No room to slide into DMs with heart emojis and stuff. Love does not vibe well with mourning bro. Her pops thinks it's a red flag that she lets herself be so sad. He thinks speed-running our "I do's" will cancel her sorrows and if she had a bae, she might find some chill. So thats the reason for the rush.

FRIAR LAURENCE

(Aside) I would I knew not why it should be slow'd.

Look, sir, here comes the lady towards my cell.

*(Enter **Juliet**)*

PARIS

Happily met, my lady and my wife!

JULIET

That may be, sir, when I may be a wife.

PARIS

That may be must be, love, on Thursday next.

JULIET

What must be shall be.

FRIAR LAURENCE

That's a certain text.

PARIS

Come you to make confession to this father?

FRIAR LAURENCE

(Under his breath) If only I didn't get why we should be pumping the brakes rn. Yo, look, here comes thy shorty now.

*(**Juliet** enters)*

PARIS

Aye, what's good, bae and future queen!

JULIET

Maybe, if it's lore accurate.

PARIS

That "maybe", "must be" come Thursday.

JULIET

It is what it is.

FRIAR LAURENCE

Facts.

PARIS

Is thou rolling up here to make a confession to the padre?

JULIET

To answer that, I should confess to you.

PARIS

Do not deny to him that you love me.

JULIET

I will confess to you that I love him.

PARIS

So will ye, I am sure, that you love me.

JULIET

If I do so, it will be of more price, being spoke behind your back, than to your face.

PARIS

Poor soul, thy face is much abused with tears.

JULIET

The tears have got small victory by that; for it was bad enough before their spite.

JULIET

To spill that tea would mean I'm confessing unto thee, right?

PARIS

Don't tell him you're sus about our love. Girl it's a match!

JULIET

Bet, I'll slide into his DMs with talk of love.

PARIS

You'll drop that in my inbox too, I bet.

JULIET

If I do, it's more real to say it behind your back than to your face.

PARIS

Poor thing, your face is taking damage from all that crying.

JULIET

Those tears didn't do much, my face was already busted.

PARIS

Thou wrong'st it, more than tears, with that report.

JULIET

That is no slander, sir, which is a truth; and what I spake, I spake it to my face.

PARIS

Thy face is mine, and thou hast slander'd it.

JULIET

It may be so, for it is not mine own. Are you at leisure, holy father, now; or shall I come to you at evening mass?

FRIAR LAURENCE

My leisure serves me, pensive daughter, now. My lord, we must entreat the time alone.

PARIS

God shield I should disturb devotion! Juliet, on Thursday early will I rouse ye: till then, adieu; and keep this holy kiss.

(Exit)

PARIS

You're wrong for that, roasting your own selfie is too extra.

JULIET

That's all real talk; my truth, no cap.

PARIS

Your selfie is my background, and thou hath just torched it!

JULIET

Might be, 'cause that selfie leaked to the wrong hands. - Yo, Friar, you got a sec now, or after mass?

FRIAR LAURENCE

I'm here for you, fam, in this troubled hour to pass. *(To **Paris**)* Bruh, we need some one-on-one time.

PARIS

Wouldn't dream of blocking her spiritual journey! Juliet, Thursday's sunrise, we shall start our forever love. *(kissing her)* Till then, stay valid!

*(**Paris** exits)*

JULIET

O shut the door! and when thou hast done so, come weep with
me; past hope, past cure, past help!

FRIAR LAURENCE

Ah, Juliet, I already know thy grief; it strains me past the compass
of my wits: I hear thou must, and nothing may prorogue it, on
Thursday next be married to this county.

JULIET

Tell me not, friar, that thou hear'st of this, unless thou tell me how
I may prevent it: if, in thy wisdom, thou canst give no help, do
thou but call my resolution wise, and with this knife I'll help it
presently. God join'd my heart and Romeo's, thou our hands; and
ere this hand, by thee to Romeo seal'd, shall be the label to
another deed, or my true heart with treacherous revolt turn to
another, this shall slay them both: therefore, out of thy long-
experienced time, give me some present counsel, or, behold, 'twixt
my extremes and me this bloody knife shall play the umpire,
arbitrating that which the commission of thy years and art could to
no issue of true honour bring. Be not so long to speak; I long to
die, if what thou speak'st speak not of remedy.

FRIAR LAURENCE

Hold, daughter: I do spy a kind of hope, which craves as
desperate an execution. As that is desperate which we would
prevent. If, rather than to marry County Paris, thou hast the
strength of will to slay thyself, then is it likely thou wilt undertake a
thing like death to chide away this shame, that copest with death
himself to scape from it: and, if thou darest, I'll give thee remedy.

JULIET

Close the door and come drown in sorrow with me! We're way
past the point of no return!

FRIAR LAURENCE

Jules, I've seen your story; thy struggle's real. They're pushing you
to change your status by Thursday, and it seems locked in.

JULIET

Don't even, unless you've got the cheat code to stop this wedding.
If thy wisdom be out of service, just hype up my plan B! *(She
whips out a knife)* And I'll hit the reset button right now with this!
Heaven linked my heart to Romeo's, and you made it official. Ill
straight up unalive myself before I cheat on my bae! You got the
XP, drop some knowledge on this messed up situation. Or just
spectate. Stuck between a rock and a sharp place, I'll be the judge
with this blade! I'm down to solve this problem if you can't fix it,
despite all your skills. Spit it out fast, 'cause if your next words ain't
a plan that slaps, I'll hit cancel on life!

FRIAR LAURENCE

Pause, girl, there's a loophole. But we gotta be bold 'cause the sitch
is critical. If you are hardcore enough to think about canceling
yourself to avoid marrying Paris, then you're game enough to fake
your own death to dodge this L. You can face off with death as a
girl boss and dip out on all this drama! And if you're really down,
I'll give thee a walkthrough.

JULIET

O, bid me leap, rather than marry Paris, from off the battlements
of yonder tower; or walk in thievish ways; or bid me lurk where
serpents are; chain me with roaring bears; or shut me nightly in a
charnel-house, O'er-cover'd quite with dead men's rattling bones,
with reeky shanks and yellow chapless skulls; or bid me go into a
new-made grave and hide me with a dead man in his shroud;
things that, to hear them told, have made me tremble; and I will
do it without fear or doubt, to live an unstain'd wife to my sweet
love.

FRIAR LAURENCE

Hold, then; go home, be merry, give consent to marry Paris:
Wednesday is to-morrow: to-morrow night look that thou lie
alone; let not thy nurse lie with thee in thy chamber: take thou this
vial, being then in bed, and this distilled liquor drink thou off;
When presently through all thy veins shall run a cold and drowsy
humour, for no pulse shall keep his native progress, but surcease:
no warmth, no breath, shall testify thou livest; the roses in thy lips
and cheeks shall fade to paly ashes, thy eyes' windows fall, like
death, when he shuts up the day of life; each part, deprived of
supple government, shall, stiff and stark and cold, appear like
death: and in this borrow'd likeness of shrunk death thou shalt
continue two and forty hours, and then awake as from a pleasant
sleep. Now, when the bridegroom in the morning comes to rouse
thee from thy bed, there art thou dead: then, as the manner of our
country is, in thy best robes uncover'd on the bier thou shalt be
borne to that same ancient vault where all the kindred of the
Capulets lie. In the mean time, against thou shalt awake, shall
Romeo by my letters know our drift, and hither shall he come:
and he and I will watch thy waking, and that very night shall
Romeo bear thee hence to Mantua. And this shall free thee from
this present shame; if no inconstant toy, nor womanish fear, abate
thy valour in the acting it.

JULIET

Tell me to yeet myself off the castle's tower, rather than walk down
the aisle to Paris! Set me up in a pit of vipers! Lock me up with
lions, tigers, and bears! Stash me in a crypt, full of creepy-crawlies
and spooky scary skeletons, frfr! Or bury me alive in some newb's
grave, snuggled up with his corpse! That all sounds like pure
nightmare fuel, but I'll run that gauntlet, no fear, no pause, just to
keep it a hundred as Romeo's one and only!

FRIAR LAURENCE

Okay chill! Head home, keep it light and play along with the Paris
plan. Tomorrow's Wednesday. Tomorrow night, make sure you're
flying solo. Don't let the nurse crash in your room.
(Showing her a vial) When you hit the bed, pop this vial, mix it up
with some drink, and down it. A cool, sleepy vibe will cruise
through your veins, and your pulse will ghost. You'll go cold, and
breathless. Your glow will fade to grey, and your eyes will crash.
You'll be like, straight-up dead! You can't even! You'll chill in this
death mode for forty-two hours, then you'll snap back like it was
just a nap. Come Thursday morning, when your boi Paris checks
in, you'll be playing dead. They'll snatch you up and set you in a
box, and you'll get a VIP pass to the Capulet crypt. Meanwhile, I'll
slide Romeo the deets. He'll show up, and we'll stake out your
revival. That night, Romeo will carry you off to Mantua. This plan
beats your current drama, as long as you don't bail or flake out and
wreck the whole plan.

JULIET

Give me, give me! O, tell not me of fear!

FRIAR LAURENCE

Hold; get you gone, be strong and prosperous in this resolve: I'll send a friar with speed to Mantua, with my letters to thy lord.

JULIET

Love give me strength! And strength shall help afford. Farewell, dear father!

(Exeunt)

JULIET

Pass that vial over here. Hand it over! Skip the scare tactics!

FRIAR LAURENCE

(Handing her the vial) Bet, Now bounce and hold it down. I'll hit
up a friar to jet with a note for Romeo.

JULIET

Love gives me strength! And strength shall help me secure this W!
Farewell, dear father!

(They exit)

ACT FOUR

SCENE TWO

*(Enter **Capulet**, **Lady Capulet**, **nurse**, and two Servingmen)*

CAPULET

So many guests invite as here are writ.

(Exit First Servant)

Sirrah, go hire me twenty cunning cooks.

SECOND SERVINGMAN

You shall have none ill, sir; for I'll try if they can lick their fingers.

CAPULET

How canst thou try them so?

SECOND SERVINGMAN

Marry, sir, 'tis an ill cook that cannot lick his own fingers: therefore he that cannot lick his fingers goes not with me.

ACT FOUR

SCENE TWO

*(**Capulet** enters with **Lady Capulet**, the **nurse**, and two servingmen)*

CAPULET

(Handing the first servingman a list) Get the RSVPs from everyone here.

(The first servingman dips out.)

(To second servingman) Yo, scout me twenty dope chefs!

SECOND SERVINGMAN

No cap, you won't catch any bad chefs coming from me. Gonna check their skills by the finger-lick test.

CAPULET

You can vet them like that?

SECOND SERVINGMAN

Straight facts, sir! If a chef can't vibe with his own cooking enough to taste it, then he ain't the one!

CAPULET

Go, be gone.

(Exit Second Servant)

We shall be much unfurnished for this time. What, is my daughter gone to Friar Laurence?

NURSE

Ay, forsooth.

CAPULET

Well, he may chance to do some good on her: a peevish self-will'd harlotry it is.

(Enter Juliet)

NURSE

See where she comes from shrift with merry look.

CAPULET

How now, my headstrong! where have you been gadding?

CAPULET

Bounce, make haste!

(Exit Second Servant)

Our prep be kinda on the edge for the 'morrow. Yo, nurse, is Juliet with the Friar?

NURSE

Sure is.

CAPULET

Bet, maybe he'll flip the script on her. She's been on one!

(Juliet slides in)

NURSE

Look, she's back from her one-on-one with a smile.

CAPULET

What's good, stubborn one? Where have you been?

JULIET

Where I have learn'd me to repent the sin of disobedient opposition to you and your behests, and am enjoin'd by holy Laurence to fall prostrate here, and beg your pardon: pardon, I beseech you! Henceforward I am ever ruled by you.

CAPULET

Send for the county; go tell him of this: I'll have this knot knit up to-morrow morning.

JULIET

I met the youthful lord at Laurence' cell; and gave him what becomed love I might, not step o'er the bounds of modesty.

CAPULET

Why, I am glad on't; this is well: stand up: this is as't should be. Let me see the county; ay, marry, go, I say, and fetch him hither. Now, afore God! this reverend holy friar, our whole city is much bound to him.

JULIET

Nurse, will you go with me into my closet, to help me sort such needful ornaments as you think fit to furnish me to-morrow?

LADY CAPULET

No, not till Thursday; there is time enough.

JULIET

Just been learning that not listening to my dad is a major no-no, and I need to vibe with your wishes. Friar Laurence Got me down to ask for a truce, so like, I'm sorry for real. From here on out your word is law.

CAPULET

Slide into the DMs of the Count. Fill him in. We're locking this thing down at sunrise.

JULIET

Linked up with the young lord at Friar Laurence's spot. Gave him all the legit feels, keeping it one hundred.

CAPULET

Aye, that's what's up, I'm feeling this! This is gonna be lit! Get up.

(*Juliet* stands up)

Good choice! I'm hyped to see the Count. Bless that dope friar, the whole city owes him props!

JULIET

Nurse, roll with me to my room, help me pick out some fresh drip for the big day.

LADY CAPULET

Chill, no rush till Thursday. We got mad time.

CAPULET

Go, nurse, go with her: we'll to church to-morrow.

(Exeunt Juliet and nurse)

LADY CAPULET

We shall be short in our provision: 'Tis now near night.

CAPULET

Tush, I will stir about, and all things shall be well, I warrant thee, wife: go thou to Juliet, help to deck up her; I'll not to bed to-night; let me alone; I'll play the housewife for this once. What, ho! They are all forth. Well, I will walk myself to County Paris, to prepare him up against to-morrow: my heart is wondrous light, since this same wayward girl is so reclaim'd.

(Exeunt)

CAPULET

Nurse, roll with her. We're doing the 'I do's' at the chapel in the A.M.

(Juliet and the nurse peace out)

LADY CAPULET

We're gonna be tight on the supplies. Night's falling.

CAPULET

No stress, I'm on it. Trust, wifey, it's gonna be lit. Go get Juliet all glammed up. I'm gonna stay up, run this house like a boss for the night.

(Lady Capulet exits)

Yo! They dipped? A'ight, bet, I'll hit the pavement to the Count Paris, get him in the loop for the morrow. My heart's doing backflips 'cause this once-troubled shorty is back in line, ready to rock that aisle.

(Capulet exits.)

ACT FOUR

SCENE THREE

(Enter Juliet and nurse)

JULIET

Ay, those attires are best: but, gentle nurse, I pray thee, leave me
to my self to-night, for I have need of many orisons to move the
heavens to smile upon my state, which, well thou know'st, is cross,
and full of sin.

(Enter Lady Capulet)

LADY CAPULET

What, are you busy, ho? need you my help?

JULIET

No, madam; we have cull'd such necessaries as are behoveful for
our state to-morrow: so please you, let me now be left alone, and
let the nurse this night sit up with you; for, I am sure, you have
your hands full all, in this so sudden business.

ACT FOUR

SCENE THREE

(Juliet and the nurse enter)

JULIET

Yeah, these fits are straight fire! But yo, nurse, I gotta fly solo tonight. Got a whole bunch of praying to do, you know my life's all twisted up, mad sins and all.

(Lady Capulet enters)

LADY CAPULET

What's poppin'? Does thou need me to do something?

JULIET

Nay mom, we got the fit on lock for the morrow. So, if you're cool with it, I wanna vibe alone. Have the nurse chill with you tonight, since you've got a lot going on with this last-min party prep.

LADY CAPULET

Good night: get thee to bed, and rest; for thou hast need.

*(Exeunt **Lady Capulet** and **nurse**)*

JULIET

Farewell! God knows when we shall meet again. I have a faint cold
fear thrills through my veins, that almost freezes up the heat of
life: I'll call them back again to comfort me: Nurse! What should
she do here? My dismal scene I needs must act alone. Come, vial.
What if this mixture do not work at all? Shall I be married then
to-morrow morning? No, no: this shall forbid it: lie thou there.
(Laying down her dagger) What if it be a poison, which the friar
subtly hath minister'd to have me dead, lest in this marriage he
should be dishonour'd, because he married me before to Romeo?
I fear it is: and yet, methinks, it should not, for he hath still been
tried a holy man. How if, when I am laid into the tomb, I wake
before the time that Romeo come to redeem me? There's a
fearful point! Shall I not, then, be stifled in the vault, to whose foul
mouth no healthsome air breathes in, and there die strangled ere
my Romeo comes?Or, if I live, is it not very like, the horrible
conceit of death and night, together with the terror of the place,--
As in a vault, an ancient receptacle, where, for these many
hundred years, the bones of all my buried ancestors are packed:
where bloody Tybalt, yet but green in earth, lies festering in his
shroud; where, as they say, at some hours in the night spirits
resort;- alack, alack, is it not like that I, so early waking, what with
loathsome smells, and shrieks like mandrakes' torn out of the
earth, that living mortals, hearing them, run mad:- O, if I wake,
shall I not be distraught, environed with all these hideous fears?
And madly play with my forefather's joints? And pluck the
mangled Tybalt from his shroud? And, in this rage, with some
great kinsman's bone, as with a club, bash out my desperate

LADY CAPULET

A'ight, nighty night! Hit the sheets and get that beauty sleep, you look like you could use it!

*(**Lady Capulet** and the **nurse** dip)*

JULIET

Peace out! Only the man upstairs knows when we'll link up again! Got this sus feeling sliding through me, practically putting my life's flame on ice! Might holler for them to come back for some comfort. Nurse! - But nay, what would she even do? In this wild situation, I gotta handle my business solo. Okay, here it goes with the potion. What if this mix is a flop? Am I gonna be stuck saying "I do" in the AM? Nah, this blade's my plan B. Just chill there. *(she sets down the knife)* What if Friar's on some shady biz and whipped up this drink to off me? Is he stressed about getting canceled if I marry Paris after his low-key wedding with me and Romeo? Got me shook thinking it might be toxic. But he is supposed to be a legit holy dude. What if I wake up in that crypt before my boy Romeo rolls in to rescue? Is that gonna be my final scene, choking out in that vault? Ain't no fresh air down there! Or what if I'm alive, all alone with the dead and the darkness? That's straight-up horror! That vault's gonna be stacked with ancient bones, and Tybalt's fresh grave. They say spirits throw hands in tombs at night. Oh no, I can't even! Waking up to those rank smells and hearing screams, that would make anyone lose their mind. If I snap out of it too early, could I legit lose my mind with all that creepy stuff around, and start messing with my fam's old bones, and yank Tybalt out of his burial gear? Could I even grab a bone from one of my long-gone kin and go all Hamlet on myself? Oh snap, I'm bugging... I swear I see Tybalt's ghost out there hunting for Romeo since Romeo put him down! Hold up, Tybalt, chill! Romeo, Romeo, Romeo! This one's for thee!

brains? O, look! methinks I see my cousin's ghost seeking out Romeo, that did spit his body upon a rapier's point: stay, Tybalt, stay! Romeo, I come! this do I drink to thee.

(She falls upon her bed, within the curtains)

(She throws back the potion and collapses onto her bed, out of sight behind the bed curtains.)

ACT FOUR

SCENE FOUR

*(Enter **Lady Capulet** and **nurse**)*

LADY CAPULET

Hold, take these keys, and fetch more spices, nurse.

NURSE

They call for dates and quinces in the pastry.

*(Enter **Capulet**)*

CAPULET

Come, stir, stir, stir! the second cock hath crow'd, the curfew-bell hath rung, 'tis three o'clock: look to the baked meats, good Angelica: spare not for the cost.

NURSE

Go, you cot-quean, go, get you to bed; faith, You'll be sick to-morrow for this night's watching.

ACT FOUR

SCENE FOUR

(Lady Capulet and the nurse enter)

LADY CAPULET

Hold up, nurse. Grab these keys and snag some more spices.

NURSE

They need dates and quinces in the pastry kitchen.

(Capulet enters)

CAPULET

Let's get moving, wake up, wake up! Dawn's already breaking. The night bell's tolled, it's three already. Angelica, make sure those meats smack, spare no cost!

NURSE

Off to bed with you, you night owl! You'll be out of sorts tomorrow after this all-nighter!

CAPULET

No, not a whit: what! I have watch'd ere now all night for lesser cause, and ne'er been sick.

LADY CAPULET

Ay, you have been a mouse-hunt in your time; but I will watch you from such watching now.

*(Exeunt **Lady Capulet** and **nurse**)*

CAPULET

A jealous hood, a jealous hood! *(Enter three or four Servingmen, with spits, logs, and baskets)*

Now, fellow, what's there?

FIRST SERVINGMAN

Things for the cook, sir; but I know not what.

CAPULET

Make haste, make haste.

(Exit First Servant)

Sirrah, fetch drier logs: call Peter, he will show thee where they are.

CAPULET

Nah, I'm solid. I've done all-nighters for way less without crashing.

LADY CAPULET

Well, thou has charmed a fair share of ladies back in the day, no cap. But no more late nights for you!

(*Lady Capulet* and the **nurse** *exit*)

CAPULET

She's just peanut butter and jealous!

(*A few servingmen come in with cooking gear*)

Alright, guys, what's in the haul?

FIRST SERVINGMAN

Stuff for the chef, sir. Couldn't tell you exactly what, though.

CAPULET

Snap to it, quickly now!

(*The first servingman exits*)

(*To second servingman*)

Bro, grab some logs that'll burn longer. Call Peter, he knows where the stash is.

SECOND SERVINGMAN

I have a head, sir, that will find out logs, and never trouble Peter for the matter.

(Exit)

CAPULET

Mass, and well said; a merry whoreson, ha! Thou shalt be logger-head. Good faith, 'tis day: the county will be here with music straight, for so he said he would: I hear him near.

(Music within)

Nurse! Wife! What, ho! What, nurse, I say!

*(Re-enter **nurse**)*

Go waken Juliet, go and trim her up; I'll go and chat with Paris: hie, make haste, make haste; the bridegroom he is come already: make haste, I say.

(Exeunt)

SECOND SERVINGMAN

I am smart enough to scout them out without Peter's help.

(The second servingman exits)

CAPULET

Bet, nice comeback, thou shall outsmart them all. It's light out already. The count will show up with his band any minute, Just like he said he would. Sounds like they're outside rn no cap.

(Music is heard in the distance)

Hey, nurse! Wife! Yo, nurse!

*(The **nurse** comes back in)*

Go get Juliet ready. I'm off to chat with Paris. Let's make it quick! The groom's already here. Hustle, I mean it!

(They all leave the stage)

ACT FOUR

SCENE FIVE

*(Enter **nurse**)*

NURSE

Mistress! what, mistress! Juliet! fast, I warrant her, she: why, lamb!
why, lady! fie, you slug-a-bed! Why, love, I say! madam! sweet-
heart! why, bride! What, not a word? you take your pennyworths
now; sleep for a week; for the next night, I warrant, the County
Paris hath set up his rest, that you shall rest but little. God forgive
me, Marry, and amen, how sound is she asleep! I must needs
wake her. Madam, madam, madam! Ay, let the county take you in
your bed; he'll fright you up, i' faith. Will it not be?

(Undraws the curtains)

What, dress'd! and in your clothes! and down again! I must needs
wake you; Lady! lady! lady! Alas, alas! Help, help! my lady's dead!
O, well-a-day, that ever I was born! Some aqua vitae, ho! My lord!
my lady!

*(Enter **Lady Capulet**)*

LADY CAPULET

What noise is here?

ACT FOUR

SCENE FIVE

*(The **nurse** enters)*

NURSE

Yo, Juliet! Girl, is thou still hitting snooze? Hey, sweetie! Hey, girl! Hey, my love, I'm talking! Queen! Hey, soon-to-be wifey! You ghosting me? You're catching all these Zs now, huh? 'Cause tomorrow night, Paris ain't gonna let you rest, bet. My bad, God! For real, she's out like a light! Gotta wake her. Madam, madam! Yeah, Paris will get a kick out of this – he'll be the one to wake you... Bet.

(She pulls back the curtains)

Wait, what? Still in your fit from yesterday? Gotta wake you, Lady! Lady! Nooo! OMG! OMG! Help, my lady's not breathing! This is the worst day ever! Someone get me a drink, stat! My lord! My lady!

*(**Lady Capulet** enters)*

LADY CAPULET

What's all this commotion?

NURSE

O lamentable day!

LADY CAPULET

What is the matter?

NURSE

Look, look! O heavy day!

LADY CAPULET

O me, O me! My child, my only life, revive, look up, or I will die with thee! Help, help! Call help.

(Enter Capulet)

CAPULET

For shame, bring Juliet forth; her lord is come.

NURSE

She's dead, deceased, she's dead; alack the day!

LADY CAPULET

Alack the day, she's dead, she's dead, she's dead!

NURSE

This day... it's literally the worst!

LADY CAPULET

What's gone down?

NURSE

Look, look! Seriously, it's all kinds of bad!

LADY CAPULET

Oh snap, oh snap! My baby, my world, open those eyes, Or I'm
going down with you! Somebody, anybody, help!

(Capulet enters)

CAPULET

Quit this scene, get Juliet out here. Her man's waiting.

NURSE

She's gone, passed on, she's dead. This day's a nightmare!

LADY CAPULET

This day's a curse! She's gone, she's legit dead!

CAPULET

Ha! let me see her: out, alas! she's cold: her blood is settled, and her joints are stiff; life and these lips have long been separated: death lies on her like an untimely frost upon the sweetest flower of all the field.

NURSE

O lamentable day!

LADY CAPULET

O woful time!

CAPULET

Death, that hath ta'en her hence to make me wail, ties up my tongue, and will not let me speak.

*(Enter **Friar Laurence** and **Paris**, with Musicians)*

FRIAR LAURENCE

Come, is the bride ready to go to church?

CAPULET

Ready to go, but never to return. O son! the night before thy wedding-day hath Death lain with thy wife. There she lies, flower as she was, deflowered by him. Death is my son-in-law, death is

CAPULET

No way! Let me see her. Oh no, she's ice! Her blood's like stopped, her body's all rigid. She's been gone for a minute. Death's frosted over the dopest flower in the field!

NURSE

This is just tragic!

LADY CAPULET

Oh, cursed day!

CAPULET

Death's gone and snatched her away, got me in my feels so hard I can't even speak!

*(**Friar Laurence** and **Paris** enter with the band)*

FRIAR LAURENCE

So, we ready to hit up the church or what?

CAPULET

She's ready to roll, but it's going to be a one-way trip. *(To **Paris**)* Bruh, the night before you were supposed to tie the knot, the Grim Reaper went and made her his bae. Look at her, man! She was in full bloom, but Death went and plucked her. That dude's now my kin. He inherited everything, man! My girl went and

my heir; my daughter he hath wedded: I will die, and leave him all; life, living, all is death's.

PARIS

Have I thought long to see this morning's face, and doth it give me such a sight as this?

LADY CAPULET

Accursed, unhappy, wretched, hateful day! Most miserable hour that e'er time saw in lasting labour of his pilgrimage! But one, poor one, one poor and loving child, but one thing to rejoice and solace in, and cruel death hath catch'd it from my sight!

NURSE

O woe! O woful, woful, woful day! Most lamentable day, most woful day, that ever, ever, I did yet behold! O day! O day! O day! O hateful day! Never was seen so black a day as this: O woful day, O woful day!

PARIS

Beguiled, divorced, wronged, spited, slain! Most detestable death, by thee beguil'd, by cruel cruel thee quite overthrown! O love! O life! not life, but love in death!

eloped with Death! Guess when I kick the bucket, I let him have
it all. My whole life, all my dough, it all belongs to Death!

PARIS

Did I seriously wait all this time, just for this nightmare?

LADY CAPULET

This day is straight cursed, I hate it! The absolute worst of times,
for real! I had just this one, my one and only, my heart, and now
death's yoinked her from me!

NURSE

This is straight agony! The most heart-wrenching, tear-jerking,
tragic day I've ever seen! Like, seriously, what even is today? Such
a cursed day! Today's nothing but pure pain, nothing but pain!

PARIS

She got played, worked, done dirty, totally wrecked! Death, that
low-key worst of the worst, fooled her! That savage Death went
and offed her! Oh, the feels! Oh, the emptiness! Ain't no life
without my boo!

CAPULET

Despised, distressed, hated, martyr'd, kill'd! Uncomfortable time, why camest thou now to murder, murder our solemnity? O child! O child! my soul, and not my child! Dead art thou! Alack! my child is dead; and with my child my joys are buried.

FRIAR LAURENCE

Peace, ho, for shame! confusion's cure lives not in these confusions. Heaven and yourself had part in this fair maid; now heaven hath all, and all the better is it for the maid: your part in her you could not keep from death, but heaven keeps his part in eternal life. The most you sought was her promotion; for 'twas your heaven she should be advanced: and weep ye now, seeing she is advanced above the clouds, as high as heaven itself? O, in this love, you love your child so ill, that you run mad, seeing that she is well: she's not well married that lives married long; but she's best married that dies married young. Dry up your tears, and stick your rosemary on this fair corse; and, as the custom is, in all her best array bear her to church: for though fond nature bids us an lament, yet nature's tears are reason's merriment.

CAPULET

All things that we ordained festival, turn from their office to black funeral; our instruments to melancholy bells, our wedding cheer to a sad burial feast, our solemn hymns to sullen dirges change, our bridal flowers serve for a buried corse, and all things change them to the contrary.

CAPULET

Loathed, wrecked, despised, the ultimate betrayal! Why'd this
have to go down now, of all times? Why'd Death have to crash thy
wedding bash? Oh, my kid! Oh, my heart! You're gone. Oh, snap!
My baby's gone, and with her, all my joy's straight-up buried as
well!

FRIAR LAURENCE

Chill out, for real! This chaos isn't solving anything. You and
Heaven both had time with this gem, and now she's got VIP
heaven access. That's a major upgrade for her. Death's high-key
inevitable, and she's got that forever glow now. You hoped she'd
rise up in the world, and now she's ascended past the clouds, for
real? You're wildin out 'cause you think she's not fine, but she's
more than fine; she just got the ultimate dub! She's not the one
who had a long marriage, but the one who left a legacy. Wipe
those tears, hold on to thy memories, dress her up, and let's honor
her right, even if our hearts are heavy, these tears are just Earth's
tribute to her spirit.

CAPULET

All our party plans gotta flip to funeral vibes, our playlist is tolling
bells, our celebration to a low-key a vigil, our anthems to somber
tunes, our floral arrangements to her last tribute. Everything's got
to flip.

FRIAR LAURENCE

Sir, go you in; and, madam, go with him; and go, Sir Paris; every one prepare to follow this fair corse unto her grave: the heavens do lour upon you for some ill; move them no more by crossing their high will.

(*Exeunt* **Capulet, Lady Capulet, Paris,** *and* **Friar Laurence**)

FIRST MUSICIAN

Faith, we may put up our pipes, and be gone.

NURSE

Honest goodfellows, ah, put up, put up; for, well you know, this is a pitiful case.

(Exit)

FIRST MUSICIAN

Ay, by my troth, the case may be amended.

(Enter **Peter***)*

PETER

Musicians, O, musicians, 'Heart's ease, Heart's ease:' O, an you will have me live, play 'Heart's ease.'

FRIAR LAURENCE

Alright, go inside, and you too, madam. Paris, my guy, let's get ready to escort her to her final drop spot. Heaven's looking down on us with some side-eye, don't make it worse by beefing with the universe.

(Capulet, Lady Capulet, Paris, and Friar Laurence exit)

FIRST MUSICIAN

Time to pack it up, the show's over.

NURSE

Straight facts, stash the instruments, boys. This is just all-around a mood.

(She exits)

FIRST MUSICIAN

Yes, things could get better.

(Peter enters)

PETER

Yo, musicians, if you want me to hold it together, hit me with "Heart's ease".

FIRST MUSICIAN

Why 'Heart's ease?'

PETER

O, musicians, because my heart itself plays 'My heart is full of woe:' O, play me some merry dump, to comfort me.

FIRST MUSICIAN

Not a dump we; 'tis no time to play now.

PETER

You will not, then?

FIRST MUSICIAN

No.

PETER

I will then give it you soundly.

FIRST MUSICIAN

What will you give us?

PETER

No money, on my faith, but the gleek; I will give you the minstrel.

FIRST MUSICIAN

Why "Heart's ease," though?

PETER

Because my internal playlist is on a loop of "My heart's breaking." So, let's switch it up, play some tracks to vibe up, you feel?

FIRST MUSICIAN

Sorry man, this isn't the right vibe for tunes right now.

PETER

Y'all really not gonna play?

FIRST MUSICIAN

Hard pass, dude.

PETER

Then I'll really give it to thee.

FIRST MUSICIAN

And what's that gonna be?

PETER

Not cash, but I'm about to straight up roast you bois!

FIRST MUSICIAN

Then I will give you the serving-creature.

PETER

Then will I lay the serving-creature's dagger on your pate. I will carry no crotchets: I'll re you, I'll fa you; do you note me?

FIRST MUSICIAN

An you re us and fa us, you note us.

SECOND MUSICIAN

Pray you, put up your dagger, and put out your wit.

PETER

Then have at you with my wit! I will dry-beat you with an iron wit, and put up my iron dagger. Answer me like men:

(Sings)

'When griping grief the heart doth wound,

And doleful dumps the mind oppress,

Then music with her silver sound'--

why 'silver sound'? why 'music with her silver

sound'? What say you, Simon Catling?

FIRST MUSICIAN

Cool, I'll clap right back at you then.

PETER

Alright, it's time for some truth. Forget music class; I'm about to drop bars, ya feel?

FIRST MUSICIAN

If you're trying to hit the right note with us, better make it quick.

SECOND MUSICIAN

Easy dude, sheathe thy sharp words and chill!

PETER

Bet! I'm gonna lay down some epic bars, and a killer hook. Now give me some back:

(Sings)

'When heavy feels strike deep,

And moody vibes weigh us down,

Why do we say 'music with her silver sound'?

How 'bout 'music with that lit energy'?

What's your vibe on that, Simon Catling?

FIRST MUSICIAN

Marry, sir, because silver hath a sweet sound.

PETER

Pretty! What say you, Hugh Rebeck?

SECOND MUSICIAN

I say 'silver sound,' because musicians sound for silver.

PETER

Pretty too! What say you, James Soundpost?

THIRD MUSICIAN

Faith, I know not what to say.

PETER

O, I cry you mercy; you are the singer: I will say for you. It is 'music with her silver sound,' because musicians have no gold for sounding: 'then music with her silver sound with speedy help doth lend redress.'

*(Exeunt **Peter**)*

FIRST MUSICIAN

What a pestilent knave is this same!

FIRST MUSICIAN

Yo, it's 'cause silvers got that clean, rich sound.

PETER

Nice one! And you, Hugh Rebeck, what's your spin?

SECOND MUSICIAN

I'm all about "silver sound" 'cause we're out here chasing that shine.

PETER

Smooth! And you, James Soundpost, spit your truth!

THIRD MUSICIAN

Dude, I'm lost for words.

PETER

Oh word, and you're the vocalist? I got you, it's "music with her silver sound", 'cause truth is, we musicians are all about that silver - that's our grind: 'Then music with her silver sound quickly brings us back when we're down.'

*(**Peter** dips)*

FIRST MUSICIAN

Man, this guy's a total trip!

SECOND MUSICIAN

Hang him, Jack! Come, we'll in here; tarry for the mourners, and stay dinner.

(Exeunt)

SECOND MUSICIAN

Let's bail on this noise! Let's hide out here; we'll wait for the crowd and score some grub.

(And they dip)

ACT FIVE

SCENE ONE

*(Enter **Romeo**)*

ROMEO

If I may trust the flattering truth of sleep, my dreams presage
some joyful news at hand: my bosom's lord sits lightly in his
throne; and all this day an unaccustom'd spirit lifts me above the
ground with cheerful thoughts. I dreamt my lady came and found
me dead--Strange dream, that gives a dead man leave to think!--
and breathed such life with kisses in my lips, that I revived, and
was an emperor. Ah me! how sweet is love itself possess'd, when
but love's shadows are so rich in joy!

*(Enter **Balthasar**)*

News from Verona!--How now, Balthasar! Dost thou not bring me
letters from the friar? How doth my lady? Is my father well? How
fares my Juliet? that I ask again; for nothing can be ill, if she be
well.

BALTHASAR

Then she is well, and nothing can be ill: her body sleeps in Capel's
monument, and her immortal part with angels lives. I saw her laid
low in her kindred's vault, and presently took post to tell it you: O,
pardon me for bringing these ill news, since you did leave it for
my office, sir.

ACT FIVE

SCENE ONE

(Romeo enters)

ROMEO

If my dreams ain't trolling me, hype news is 'bout to drop. Love has my heart on lock, and all day I've felt this strange vibe. Dreamt my girl rolled up on me dead. Wild dream, right? But she hit me with a kiss and, yo, I was back, just like that. Whoa! To actually be with my bae... Just daydreaming 'bout her is pure joy.

*(Enter **Balthasar**, Romeo's homie)*

Yo, Balthasar, got any deets from Verona? Hit me up with news, man. You got a DM from the friar? How's my queen? My old man okay? Is Juliet okay? I gotta know my girl's a'ight!

BALTHASAR

All's straight, then. Her body's just catching Z's in the Capulet vault, soul's up with the angels. Caught her funeral myself, then yeeted down here to fill you in. My bad for the downer, dude, but you said that's the drill.

ROMEO

Is it even so? then I defy you, stars! Thou know'st my lodging: get me ink and paper, and hire post-horses; I will hence to-night.

BALTHASAR

I do beseech you, sir, have patience: your looks are pale and wild, and do import some misadventure.

ROMEO

Tush, thou art deceived: leave me, and do the thing I bid thee do. Hast thou no letters to me from the friar?

BALTHASAR

No, my good lord.

ROMEO

No matter: get thee gone, and hire those horses; I'll be with thee straight.

*(Exit **Balthasar**)*

Well, Juliet, I will lie with thee to-night. Let's see for means: O mischief, thou art swift to enter in the thoughts of desperate men! I do remember an apothecary,--And hereabouts he dwells,--which late I noted in tatter'd weeds, with overwhelming brows, culling of simples; meagre were his looks, sharp misery had worn him to the bones: and in his needy shop a tortoise hung, an alligator stuff'd, and other skins of ill-shaped fishes; and about his shelves a beggarly account of empty boxes, green earthen pots, bladders and musty seeds, remnants of packthread and old cakes of roses,

ROMEO

For real? Then screw you fate! Fetch me some ink and scrolls, and lock in some rides for us! I'm bouncin' to Verona tonight!

BALTHASAR

Dude, please just take a sec. You're looking all kinds of shook. Don't snap.

ROMEO

Nay, you got it twisted. Bounce and get those things done! The friar slide into your DMs?

BALTHASAR

Negative, bro.

ROMEO

Bet. Do your thing and score those horses. I'm right behind you.

(Balthasar dips out)

Yo, Juliet, I shall crash with thee tonight! Gotta figure out how – oh, the shady thoughts hit different for a desperate guy! No cap. I 'member this one dude, an apothecary— around here he chills— saw him recently dressed down in rags, brows all kinds of fierce, picking out herbs, slinging potions, life's been harsh, it's eaten him up. His shop's got this tortoise shell and some taxidermy going on, plus a bunch of empty boxes, clay pots, and some stale seeds. It's like a display of nothingness. Spotted all this and thought, "Yo, if someone needed to get their hands on some poison"—which is totally illegal here in Mantua—"this guy would be desperate enough were thinly scatter'd, to make up a show. Noting this penury, to myself I said 'An if a man did need a poison now, whose sale is present death in Mantua, here lives a caitiff wretch would sell it him.' O, this same thought did but forerun my need; and this same needy man must sell it me. As I remember, this should be the house. Being holiday, the beggar's shop is shut. What, ho! apothecary!

*(Enter **Apothecary**)*

APOTHECARY

Who calls so loud?

ROMEO

Come hither, man. I see that thou art poor: hold, there is forty ducats: let me have a dram of poison, such soon-speeding gear as will disperse itself through all the veins that the life-weary taker may fall dead and that the trunk may be discharged of breath as violently as hasty powder fired doth hurry from the fatal cannon's womb.

APOTHECARY

Such mortal drugs I have; but Mantua's law ss death to any he that utters them.

ROMEO

Art thou so bare and full of wretchedness, and fear'st to die? famine is in thy cheeks, need and oppression starveth in thine

to sell." And isn't it wild? I was just thinking about it, and now I need it. This has gotta be his place. Figures the place is closed—it's a holiday. Yo, Mr. Pharmacist!

*(The **Apothecary** comes through)*

APOTHECARY

Who's yellin' like that?

ROMEO

Slide over here, dude. I see you're hitting rough times. Here's forty bucks. I need a poison, the kind that works quick.

APOTHECARY

Got that deadly stuff, for sure. But slinging that in Mantua's a one-way ticket to the grave, man!

ROMEO

So, you're broke and beat and still scared of the end? I can see it in your face—you're hungry, man. It's obvious you're struggling.

eyes, contempt and beggary hangs upon thy back; the world is not thy friend nor the world's law; the world affords no law to make thee rich; then be not poor, but break it, and take this.

APOTHECARY

My poverty, but not my will, consents.

ROMEO

I pay thy poverty, and not thy will.

APOTHECARY

Put this in any liquid thing you will, and drink it off; and, if you had the strength of twenty men, it would dispatch you straight.

ROMEO

There is thy gold, worse poison to men's souls, doing more murders in this loathsome world, than these poor compounds that thou mayst not sell. I sell thee poison; thou hast sold me none. Farewell: buy food, and get thyself in flesh. Come, cordial and not poison, go with me to Juliet's grave; for there must I use thee.

(Exeunt)

The world's not thy bro, and the law's not thy fan. The law's not about making us rich. So, forget being broke! Take the cash, dude! *(He flashes money)*

APOTHECARY

I'm only saying yes 'cause I'm out of options, not 'cause I'm down with it.

ROMEO

I'm dropping you this cash 'cause you need it, not 'cause you're into this deal.

APOTHECARY

*(Tosses **Romeo** the poison)* Mix this with whatever. Drink it down, and even if you were as strong as twenty dudes, it'd drop you, like, instantly.

ROMEO

(Handing over the cash) Here's your paper. Money is the real poison out here, does more damage in this messed-up world than your under-the-counter stuff ever could. I just copped some poison. You didn't sell me anything. Peace out. Go treat yourself, fill out a bit. This here's a cure, not a curse, heading to Juliet's resting spot. That's where I gotta use it.

(He heads out)

ACT FIVE

SCENE TWO

*(Enter **Friar John**)*

FRIAR JOHN

Holy Franciscan friar! brother, ho!

*(Enter **Friar Laurence**)*

FRIAR LAURENCE

This same should be the voice of Friar John. Welcome from Mantua: what says Romeo? Or, if his mind be writ, give me his letter.

FRIAR JOHN

Going to find a bare-foot brother out one of our order, to associate me, here in this city visiting the sick, and finding him, the searchers of the town, suspecting that we both were in a house where the infectious pestilence did reign, seal'd up the doors, and would not let us forth; so that my speed to Mantua there was stay'd.

ACT FIVE

SCENE TWO

*(**Friar John** rolls in)*

FRIAR JOHN

Yo, holy bro, what's good?

*(**Friar Laurence** steps in)*

FRIAR LAURENCE

Yo, that's gotta be Friar John. Back from Mantua, huh? Spit the news, man! What's up with Romeo? Or, if he slid into your DMs, pass me his message.

FRIAR JOHN

Was tryna link up with a bro from our squad, found him, checking on the sick peeps here. But then, the town health peeps got sus, thinking we were chilling in a plague hotspot. They locked us in quarantine, no exit, bro! Got straight-up stuck, no chance to bounce to Mantua.

FRIAR LAURENCE

Who bare my letter, then, to Romeo?

FRIAR JOHN

I could not send it,--here it is again, Nor get a messenger to bring it thee, so fearful were they of infection.

FRIAR LAURENCE

Unhappy fortune! By my brotherhood, the letter was not nice but full of charge of dear import, and the neglecting it may do much danger. Friar John, go hence; get me an iron crow, and bring it straight unto my cell.

FRIAR JOHN

Brother, I'll go and bring it thee.

(Exit)

FRIAR LAURENCE

Now must I to the monument alone; within three hours will fair Juliet wake: she will beshrew me much that Romeo hath had no notice of these accidents; but I will write again to Mantua, and keep her at my cell till Romeo come; poor living corse, closed in a dead man's tomb!

(Exit)

FRIAR LAURENCE

Bro, who delivered my note to Romeo then?

FRIAR JOHN

Couldn't send it, fam. Got it right here. *(Hands over the letter)*
Couldn't find anyone to courier it either. Everybody's tripping
about the virus.

FRIAR LAURENCE

Dang, that's messed up! That letter was key, not just some random
DM! Ignoring it could start some real drama! Friar John, go do
me a solid; grab me a crowbar and bring it back here, ASAP!

FRIAR JOHN

Gotcha, bro. I'm on it!

(He dips out)

FRIAR LAURENCE

Looks like it's a solo mission to Juliet's resting place. She's gonna
clock in from her fake death in like three hours, and she'll be
hella mad Romeo's out of the loop. Gonna pen another note to
Mantua, and I'll keep her with me till Romeo rolls up. Poor girl's
playing dead in the crypt, what a nightmare!

(He exits, on a mission)

ACT FIVE

SCENE THREE

*(Enter **Paris**, and his **page** bearing flowers and a torch)*

PARIS

Give me thy torch, boy: hence, and stand aloof: yet put it out, for I would not be seen. Under yond yew trees lay thee all along, olding thine ear close to the hollow ground; so shall no foot upon the churchyard tread, being loose, unfirm, with digging up of graves, but thou shalt hear it: whistle then to me, as signal that thou hear'st something approach. give me those flowers. Do as I bid thee, go.

PAGE

(Aside) I am almost afraid to stand alone here in the churchyard; yet I will adventure.

(Retires)

ACT FIVE

SCENE THREE

*(**Paris** enters with his **page**)*

PARIS

Yo, dip out and keep it on the DL. Kill the light, so I won't be spotted. Post up behind those yew trees. Keep your ears open, if anyone rolls up, hit me with a whistle to give me the heads up. Pass me those flowers. Do as you're told, Bounce!

*(**Page** extinguishes torch, gives **Paris** flowers)*

PAGE

(Under his breath) Not gonna lie, kinda sketched out being solo here in the graveyard, but I'mma risk it.

*(The **page** steps aside)*

PARIS

Sweet flower, with flowers thy bridal bed I strew, O woe! Thy
canopy is dust and stones; which with sweet water nightly I will
dew, or, wanting that, with tears distill'd by moans: the obsequies
that I for thee will keep nightly shall be to strew thy grave and
weep.

*(The **page** whistles)*

The boy gives warning something doth approach. What cursed
foot wanders this way to-night, to cross my obsequies and true
love's rite? What with a torch! muffle me, night, awhile.

(Retires)

*(Enter **Romeo** and **Balthasar**)*

ROMEO

Give me that mattock and the wrenching iron. Hold, take this
letter; early in the morning see thou deliver it to my lord and
father. Give me the light: upon thy life, I charge thee, whate'er
thou hear'st or seest, stand all aloof, and do not interrupt me in
my course. Why I descend into this bed of death, is partly to
behold my lady's face; but chiefly to take thence from her dead
finger A precious ring, a ring that I must use in dear employment:
therefore hence, be gone: but if thou, jealous, dost return to pry in
what I further shall intend to do, by heaven, I will tear thee joint
by joint and strew this hungry churchyard with thy limbs: the time
and my intents are savage-wild, more fierce and more inexorable
far than empty tigers or the roaring sea.

BALTHASAR

I will be gone, sir, and not trouble you.

PARIS

(Scattering flowers on Juliet's tomb) Yo, sweet girl, I'm laying down flowers on your bridal bed. This is wild! Your cover's just dirt and rocks now. I'll keep these flowers fresh with water every night. Or if I don't, my nightly vibe will be just dropping flowers and shedding tears here.

(The page whistles)

Dang, the kid's giving me the signal! Who's creeping around here messing up my love tribute? It's someone with a torch! I gotta ghost for a sec.

(Paris ducks into the shadows)

(Romeo and Balthasar roll up)

ROMEO

Pass me that pickaxe and the crowbar. *(He grabs them from Balthasar)* Here, take this note. In the AM, make sure it gets to my pops. *(He hands over the letter to Balthasar)* Now, the light. *(He takes the torch from Balthasar)* On your life, bro, don't get nosy, whatever you see or hear, stay out of my business and don't mess with my mission. I'm 'bout to hit up this tomb, partly to see my girl one last time. But the real deal, I gotta snag this ring off her cold finger. I need it for the next hustle. So, do your thing and get gone. But if you get all sus and come back to spy, on God, I'll go beast mode on you, and turn this hungry graveyard into a Balthasar buffet. My mind's on some wild stuff right now, more savage than a starving tiger or the wildest ocean!

BALTHASAR

I'm out, no cap. Won't cause any drama!

ROMEO

So shalt thou show me friendship. Take thou that: live, and be prosperous: and farewell, good fellow.

BALTHASAR

(Aside) For all this same, I'll hide me hereabout: his looks I fear, and his intents I doubt.

(Retires)

ROMEO

Thou detestable maw, thou womb of death, gorged with the dearest morsel of the earth, thus I enforce thy rotten jaws to open, and, in despite, I'll cram thee with more food! *(Opens the tomb)*

PARIS

This is that banish'd haughty Montague, that murder'd my love's cousin, with which grief, it is supposed, the fair creature died; and here is come to do some villanous shame to the dead bodies: I will apprehend him. *(Comes forward)* Stop thy unhallow'd toil, vile Montague! Can vengeance be pursued further than death? Condemned villain, I do apprehend thee: obey, and go with me; for thou must die.

ROMEO

Bet, you're a real one for that. Take this for the road. *(He hands* **Balthasar** *some cash)* Keep it real fam.

BALTHASAR

(Under his breath so only **Paris** *can hear)* Even though I'm bailing, I'mma lurk close. Dudes got a wild look, I'm mad sus about what he's up to.

*(**Balthasar** dips out of sight and dozes off)*

ROMEO

(To the tomb) Yo, grim entrance of death! You've swallowed the GOAT. Now I'm 'bout to pry open your jaws again to bring another guest. *(Starts working on opening the tomb)*

PARIS

Isn't this that canceled Montague, the one who clapped my love's cousin, leading to her RIP, and now he's here to disrespect the dead? I'll catch him in the act. *(Steps up)* Chill with your cursed digging, foul Montague! Come to take more revenge, even after the grave? Caught red-handed, I'm bringing you in: roll with me, it shall be death for you!

ROMEO

I must indeed; and therefore came I hither. Good gentle youth,
tempt not a desperate man; fly hence, and leave me: think upon
these gone; let them affright thee. I beseech thee, youth, put not
another sin upon my head, by urging me to fury: O, be gone! By
heaven, I love thee better than myself; for I come hither arm'd
against myself: stay not, be gone; live, and hereafter say, a
madman's mercy bade thee run away.

PARIS

I do defy thy conjurations, and apprehend thee for a felon here.

ROMEO

Wilt thou provoke me? then have at thee, boy!

(They fight)

PAGE

O Lord, they fight! I will go call the watch.

(Exit)

PARIS

O, I am slain! *(Falls)* If thou be merciful, open the tomb, lay me
with Juliet. *(Dies)*

ROMEO

For real, that's why I'm here! Chill bro, don't test a desperate soul. Fall back and leave! Remember those resting in peace and let that spook you instead of me! Don't make me to go off, just bounce. I swear, I got more love for you than I do myself – I'm here on a solo mission against myself. So, dip out, stay safe, and later you can say a wild one let you live!

PARIS

Nah, I'm not buying it. You're getting booked, fam!

ROMEO

You wanna throw hands? Bet let's go!

(They throw down)

PAGE

Oh snap, it's going down! I gotta alert the squad.

*(The **page** exits, to get help)*

PARIS

I'm hit! *(He drops)* Be a real one, crack open the tomb and let me slide next to Juliet. *(He dies)*

ROMEO

In faith, I will. Let me peruse this face. Mercutio's kinsman, noble
County Paris! What said my man, when my betossed soul did not
attend him as we rode? I think he told me Paris should have
married Juliet: said he not so? or did I dream it so? Or am I mad,
hearing him talk of Juliet, to think it was so? O, give me thy hand,
one writ with me in sour misfortune's book! I'll bury thee in a
triumphant grave; a grave? O no! a lantern, slaughter'd youth, for
here lies Juliet, and her beauty makes this vault a feasting presence
full of light. Death, lie thou there, by a dead man interr'd.

*(Laying **Paris** in the tomb)*

How oft when men are at the point of death have they been
merry! which their keepers call a lightning before death: O, how
may I call this a lightning? O my love! my wife! Death, that hath
suck'd the honey of thy breath, hath had no power yet upon thy
beauty: thou art not conquer'd; beauty's ensign yet is crimson in
thy lips and in thy cheeks, and death's pale flag is not advanced
there. Tybalt, liest thou there in thy bloody sheet? O, what more
favour can I do to thee, than with that hand that cut thy youth in
twain to sunder his that was thine enemy? Forgive me, cousin! Ah,
dear Juliet, why art thou yet so fair? shall I believe that
unsubstantial death is amorous, and that the lean abhorred
monster keeps thee here in dark to be his paramour? For fear of
that, I still will stay with thee; and never from this palace of dim
night depart again: here, here will I remain with worms that are
thy chamber-maids; O, here will I set up my everlasting rest, and
shake the yoke of inauspicious stars from this world-wearied flesh.
Eyes, look your last! Arms, take your last embrace! and, lips, O
you the doors of breath, seal with a righteous kiss a dateless
bargain to engrossing death! Come, bitter conduct, come,
unsavoury guide! Thou desperate pilot, now at once run on the
dashing rocks thy sea-sick weary bark! Here's to my love! *(Drinks)*
O true apothecary! Thy drugs are quick. Thus with a kiss I die.

(Dies)

ROMEO

Bet, I got you. Gotta peep this face though. Yo, it's Mercutio's cuz, Count Paris! What was my homie saying? Wasn't really listening while we were cruisin'. He said something about Paris and Juliet getting hitched, right? Or was I just trippin'? Did I get it twisted? Yo, gimme your hand, bro. We're both straight-up unlucky. I'll lay you down.

*(**Romeo** reveals **Juliet** inside the tomb)*

Nah, this isn't just a grave. Juliet's glow turns this place bright! Other dead dudes, make room. You're getting bunked by another gone too soon. *(Lays **Paris** in the tomb)* How come dudes always feel chill before they drop? They say it's called lightness before death. But how can I hype this up? Oh man, my girl, my wifey! Death's been greedy with your vibe but couldn't touch your beauty. You ain't beat yet. Still got that blush in your cheeks and lips. Death hasn't ghosted you. Tybalt, you here in your bloodied threads? What better gift can I give you than to drop the dude who sent you off too soon? My bad, cuz! Oh, Juliet, why you gotta be looking so fire still? I know death's crushing on you too, keeping you here as his boo! Nah, I'm not with that! I'll kick it here with you; and I ain't never leaving this crib of shadows! Right here, right now, I'm setting up my forever spot, gonna shake off this unlucky curse from my tired soul. Eyes, take one last look! Arms, get your last hug! And lips, yo, you the gates of breath, seal it with a legit kiss. A timeless deal with greedy death! Let's yeet this tired vessel straight into the rocks! To us, my love! *(**Romeo** takes one last shot for love)* Dang, that dealer wasn't lying! This stuff hits fast. So, with a kiss, I'm out.

*(**Romeo** dies)*

*(**Friar Laurence** enters with a lantern, crowbar, and shovel)*

FRIAR LAURENCE

Saint Francis be my speed! how oft to-night have my old feet
stumbled at graves! Who's there?

BALTHASAR

Here's one, a friend, and one that knows you well.

FRIAR LAURENCE

Bliss be upon you! Tell me, good my friend, what torch is yond,
that vainly lends his light to grubs and eyeless skulls? as I discern,
it burneth in the Capel's monument.

BALTHASAR

It doth so, holy sir; and there's my master, one that you love.

FRIAR LAURENCE

Who is it?

BALTHASAR

Romeo.

*(**Friar Laurence** enters with a lantern, crowbar, and shovel)*

FRIAR LAURENCE

Yo, Saint Francis, give me a hand! Been tripping over gravestones all night. Who's out there?

BALTHASAR

It's me, a bro who knows you.

FRIAR LAURENCE

Bless up! Dude, what's with that light flickering over there? Just shining for the dead or what?

BALTHASAR

Facts, holy bro; and that's my boss, one whom you're down with.

FRIAR LAURENCE

Who? Romeo?

BALTHASAR

Yeah, Romeo.

FRIAR LAURENCE

How long hath he been there?

BALTHASAR

Full half an hour.

FRIAR LAURENCE

Go with me to the vault.

BALTHASAR

I dare not, sir my master knows not but I am gone hence; and fearfully did menace me with death, if I did stay to look on his intents.

FRIAR LAURENCE

Stay, then; I'll go alone. Fear comes upon me: O, much I fear some ill unlucky thing.

BALTHASAR

As I did sleep under this yew-tree here, I dreamt my master and another fought, and that my master slew him.

FRIAR LAURENCE

He's been there how long?

BALTHASAR

Like, thirty minutes, maybe.

FRIAR LAURENCE

Let's roll to the tomb.

BALTHASAR

No can do, sir. The boss man didn't want me sticking around. Said I'd catch hands if I did.

FRIAR LAURENCE

A'ight, post up here. I got a bad feeling. I'll check it out solo.

BALTHASAR

When I was catching Zs by that tree, I had this wild dream that my boss and some dude where throwing hands, and my boss murked him!

FRIAR LAURENCE

Romeo! *(Advances)* Alack, alack, what blood is this, which stains the stony entrance of this sepulchre? What mean these masterless and gory swords to lie discolour'd by this place of peace? *(Enters the tomb)* Romeo! O, pale! Who else? what, Paris too? And steep'd in blood? Ah, what an unkind hour is guilty of this lamentable chance! The lady stirs.

*(**Juliet** wakes)*

JULIET

O comfortable friar! where is my lord? I do remember well where I should be, and there I am. Where is my Romeo?

(Noise within)

FRIAR LAURENCE

I hear some noise. Lady, come from that nest of death, contagion, and unnatural sleep: a greater power than we can contradict hath thwarted our intents. Come, come away. Thy husband in thy bosom there lies dead; and Paris too. Come, I'll dispose of thee among a sisterhood of holy nuns: stay not to question, for the watch is coming; come, go, good Juliet, (Noise again) I dare no longer stay.

JULIET

Go, get thee hence, for I will not away.

*(Exit **Friar Laurence**)*

FRIAR LAURENCE

(Approaching the tomb) Romeo! Oh snap! Why is there blood all over the entrance? And who just ditched these swords? No way... *(Peeks inside)* Oh man, Romeo looks... and Paris too? All bloodied up. Yo, when did this all go down? Hold up, she's moving!

*(**Juliet** wakes)*

JULIET

Yo, Friar, where's my bae? I know I'm supposed to be here, and here I am! But where's Romeo?

(A noise echoes outside the tomb)

FRIAR LAURENCE

Yo, I hear something. Lady, you gotta bounce! Something bigger than us wrecked the game plan! Your man's out, and Paris too! Let's get you to a nunnery, no time for Q&A. We gotta dip, the cops are coming! Let's ghost, Juliet! I can't stick around!

JULIET

Bail, I'm not going anywhere!

*(**Friar Laurence** books it outta there)*

What's here? a cup, closed in my true love's hand? Poison, I see, hath been his timeless end: O churl! drunk all, and left no friendly drop To help me after? I will kiss thy lips; Haply some poison yet doth hang on them, to make die with a restorative. *(Kisses him)* Thy lips are warm.

(Enter **watchman** *and* **Paris's page***)*

HEAD WATCHMAN

(Within) Lead, boy: which way?

JULIET

Yea, noise? then I'll be brief. O happy dagger! *(Snatching Romeo's dagger)* This is thy sheath;

(Stabs herself) there rust, and let me die.

(Falls on **Romeo's** *body, and dies)*

PAGE

This is the place; there, where the torch doth burn.

HEAD WATCHMAN

The ground is bloody; search about the churchyard: go, some of you, whoe'er you find attach. Pitiful sight! here lies the county slain, and Juliet bleeding, warm, and newly dead, who here hath lain these two days buried. Go, tell the prince: run to the Capulets: raise up the Montagues: some others search: we see the ground

Now what's this? A cup in my boo's hand? Poison, frfr? That's what did him in? He selfishly sipped it all. Left none for me. Imma kiss these lips, maybe catch a deadly drop. *(She kisses **Romeo***) Lips still warm, though.

*(**Watchmen** and **Paris's page** roll up)*

HEAD WATCHMAN

*(To the **page**)* Lead the way, kid! Where to?

JULIET

What's that noise? Bet, I gotta do this fast. Oh snap, a dagger! This will be your new home, get cozy in my body, let's end this! *(She stabs herself with **Romeo's** dagger, and dies)*

PAGE

This is the spot, over here by the burning torch.

HEAD WATCHMAN

The scene's a mess, blood everywhere. Search the whole yard. Take in anyone you find.

*(Some **watchmen** exit to do just that)*

This looks rough. The count's down! Juliet's bleeding out! She's still warm, even though she's been in the ground for two days. Someone hit up the prince! Get to the Capulets, wake up the Montagues, and get more people to look around!

whereon these woes do lie; but the true ground of all these piteous woes we cannot without circumstance descry.

*(Re-enter some of the watch, with **Balthasar**)*

SECOND WATCHMAN

Here's Romeo's man; we found him in the churchyard.

HEAD WATCHMAN

Hold him in safety, till the prince come hither.

*(Re-enter others of the watch, with **Friar Laurence**)*

THIRD WATCHMAN

Here is a friar, that trembles, sighs and weeps: we took this mattock and this spade from him, as he was coming from this churchyard side.

HEAD WATCHMAN

A great suspicion: stay the friar too.

*(Enter the **prince** and Attendants)*

*(Another **watchman** exits)*

We got a glimpse of what went down, but we need the full deets to piece it all together.

*(The **second watchman** comes back with **Balthasar** in tow)*

SECOND WATCHMAN

Found Romeo's right-hand guy over here in the graveyard.

HEAD WATCHMAN

Cool, hold him until the prince shows up.

*(Then the **third watchman** comes back with **Friar Laurence**)*

THIRD WATCHMAN

Caught this friar looking all kinds of shook, crying and stuff. Took this pick and shovel off him; he was coming from over there.

HEAD WATCHMAN

Sketchy... Let's keep an eye on the friar too.

*(The **prince** rolls in with his crew)*

PRINCE

What misadventure is so early up, that calls our person from our morning's rest?

(Enter Capulet, Lady Capulet, and others)

CAPULET

What should it be, that they so shriek abroad?

LADY CAPULET

The people in the street cry Romeo, some Juliet, and some Paris; and all run, with open outcry toward our monument.

PRINCE

What fear is this which startles in our ears?

HEAD WATCHMAN

Sovereign, here lies the County Paris slain; and Romeo dead; and Juliet, dead before, warm and new kill'd.

PRINCE

Search, seek, and know how this foul murder comes.

PRINCE

What kind of mess has me up at this ungodly hour?

*(**Capulet** and **Lady Capulet** join the scene)*

CAPULET

Yo, what's got everyone out here screaming?

LADY CAPULET

Streets are buzzing with Romeo, some shout for Juliet, and others for Paris; everyone's heading to our family's monument, making noise.

PRINCE

So, what's the major drama?

HEAD WATCHMAN

Your Highness, we got Paris down. Romeo too. And Juliet, she was cold, but now she's warm. Hasn't been gone long.

PRINCE

We need to dig into this, find out what went down.

HEAD WATCHMAN

Here is a friar, and slaughter'd Romeo's man; with instruments upon them, fit to open these dead men's tombs.

CAPULET

O heavens! O wife, look how our daughter bleeds! This dagger hath mista'en--for, lo, his house is empty on the back of Montague, and it mis-sheathed in my daughter's bosom!

LADY CAPULET

O me! this sight of death is as a bell, that warns my old age to a sepulchre.

*(Enter **Montague** and others)*

PRINCE

Come, Montague; for thou art early up, to see thy son and heir more early down.

MONTAGUE

Alas, my liege, my wife is dead to-night; grief of my son's exile hath stopp'd her breath: what further woe conspires against mine age?

HEAD WATCHMAN

Here's the friar, and the dead guy's sidekick. Found 'em with the kind of gear you'd use to break into tombs!

CAPULET

Lord above! Wife, check out our kid... She's bleeding out! That dagger's supposed to be in Montague's back, not planted in our girl!

LADY CAPULET

This is too much, like a death telling me I'm next to hit the grave!

(*Montague* shows up)

PRINCE

Montague, you're here bright and early to see your kid for the last time!

MONTAGUE

Sire, my heart's heavy tonight. My lady died over the grief of our son's banishment. What's next for me in these twilight years?

PRINCE

Look, and thou shalt see.

MONTAGUE

O thou untaught! what manners is in this? To press before thy father to a grave?

PRINCE

Seal up the mouth of outrage for a while, till we can clear these ambiguities, and know their spring, their head, their true descent; and then will I be general of your woes, and lead you even to death: meantime forbear, and let mischance be slave to patience. Bring forth the parties of suspicion.

FRIAR LAURENCE

I am the greatest, able to do least, yet most suspected, as the time and place doth make against me of this direful murder; and here I stand, both to impeach and purge myself condemned and myself excused.

PRINCE

Then say at once what thou dost know in this.

FRIAR LAURENCE

I will be brief, for my short date of breath is not so long as is a tedious tale. Romeo, there dead, was husband to that Juliet; and she, there dead, that Romeo's faithful wife: I married them; and

PRINCE

Check it out for yourself.

MONTAGUE

*(Seeing **Romeo's** body)* Oh, my boy, what have you done? Skipping ahead of your old man to the grave, huh?

PRINCE

Easy now, hold off on the drama. We gotta piece this together first, figure out how it all kicked off. I'll be the one to guide you through this pain, maybe all the way to the bitter end. Just chill for now. Get me the suspects.

FRIAR LAURENCE

I did the most I could, but it turned out the least. I'm the prime suspect, since I was on the scene. I stand before you ready for your questions and the consequences. I've judged myself already, for better or worse.

PRINCE

Spill the beans, Friar. What went down here?

FRIAR LAURENCE

I'll keep it one hundred, 'cause I'm not about to cap! Romeo over there, dead, was Juliet's man. And she, also dead, was loyal to Romeo, no cap! I married them on the DL, and their secret wedding day was the day Tybalt got iced, which got Romeo exiled,

their stol'n marriage-day was Tybalt's dooms-day, whose untimely
death banish'd the new-made bridegroom from the city, for
whom, and not for Tybalt, Juliet pined. You, to remove that siege
of grief from her, betroth'd and would have married her perforce
to County Paris: then comes she to me, and, with wild looks, bid
me devise some mean to rid her from this second marriage, or in
my cell there would she kill herself. Then gave I her, so tutor'd by
my art, a sleeping potion; which so took effect as I intended, for it
wrought on her the form of death: meantime I writ to Romeo, that
he should hither come as this dire night, to help to take her from
her borrow'd grave, being the time the potion's force should cease.
But he which bore my letter, Friar John, was stay'd by accident,
and yesternight return'd my letter back. Then all alone at the
prefixed hour of her waking, came I to take her from her
kindred's vault; meaning to keep her closely at my cell, till I
conveniently could send to Romeo: but when I came, some
minute ere the time of her awaking, here untimely lay the noble
Paris and true Romeo dead. She wakes; and I entreated her come
forth, and bear this work of heaven with patience: but then a noise
did scare me from the tomb; and she, too desperate, would not go
with me, but, as it seems, did violence on herself. All this I know;
and to the marriage her nurse is privy: and, if aught in this
miscarried by my fault, let my old life be sacrificed, some hour
before his time, unto the rigour of severest law.

PRINCE

We still have known thee for a holy man. Where's Romeo's man?
What can he say in this?

that's who Juliet was really missing! You were trying to get her to forget him by pushing her to marry Paris: but she wasn't having it, came to me all wild-eyed, begging for a way out, said she'd end it in my cell if I didn't help. So, I cooked up a fake death potion, and it worked just like I planned, made her seem dead. I sent word to Romeo to be here on this tragic night, to lift her from her fake grave once the potion wore off. But the guy carrying my message got held up, and just last night, he bounced back with my letter. So, I went alone to scoop her up from her family's tomb; I planned to hide her in my cell until I could holla at Romeo, but when I got there, a bit before the wake-up time, there lay Paris and Romeo, both dead, no cap. She woke up; I tried to calm her down, told her to take this heavy scene chill, but then some noise freaked me out, and I bailed from the tomb. She was too wild to come with me, looks like she went and unalived herself. I know all this 'cause I was there. The nurse knew about the secret wedding too. If any of this went sideways 'cause of me, I am ready to take the hit, even if it means ending my time early, at the hands of the toughest justice!

PRINCE

We've always known you as a man of God. Where's Romeo's homie? What's he got to say about all this?

BALTHASAR

I brought my master news of Juliet's death; and then in post he
came from Mantua to this same place, to this same monument.
This letter he early bid me give his father, and threatened me with
death, going in the vault, I departed not and left him there.

PRINCE

Give me the letter; I will look on it. Where is the county's page,
that raised the watch? Sirrah, what made your master in this
place?

PAGE

He came with flowers to strew his lady's grave; and bid me stand
aloof, and so I did: anon comes one with light to ope the tomb;
and by and by my master drew on him; and then I ran away to call
the watch.

PRINCE

This letter doth make good the friar's words, their course of love,
the tidings of her death: and here he writes that he did buy a
poison of a poor 'pothecary, and therewithal came to this vault to
die, and lie with Juliet. Where be these enemies? Capulet!
Montague! See, what a scourge is laid upon your hate, that heaven
finds means to kill your joys with love. And I for winking at your
discords too have lost a brace of kinsmen: all are punish'd.

CAPULET

O brother Montague, give me thy hand: this is my daughter's
jointure, for no more can I demand.

BALTHASAR

I hit up my master with the news about Juliet's death, then he jetted from Mantua to this spot. *(Shows a letter)* This morning, he was like, "Give this to my dad." When he dipped into the tomb, he was like, "Bail or you're dead!"

PRINCE

Lemme see that note. *(Takes the letter from **Balthasar**)* And where's the youngin' who sounded the alarm? Kid, what was your boss up to here?

PAGE

He came to lay flowers on his chick's grave. Told me to keep my distance, which I did. Then some guy with a torch showed up to crack open the tomb, and my master was ready to throw down. I booked it to get the watch.

PRINCE

(Checks out the letter) This note's backing up what the friar said. Talks about their love story and how he got the deets on her death. Says here he copped some poison from a broke apothecary to come here and end it with Juliet. Where's the Capulet and Montague crew at? You peep the mess that comes from all this hate? Even I slept on your beef, and now my own fam are gone! We're all catching the fallout!

CAPULET

Yo, Montague, let's squash this! Peace is all I can ask for at this point!

MONTAGUE

But I can give thee more: for I will raise her statue in pure gold;
that while Verona by that name is known, there shall no figure at
such rate be set as that of true and faithful Juliet.

CAPULET

As rich shall Romeo's by his lady's lie; poor sacrifices of our
enmity!

PRINCE

A glooming peace this morning with it brings; the sun, for sorrow,
will not show his head: go hence, to have more talk of these sad
things; some shall be pardon'd, and some punished: for never was
a story of more woe than this of Juliet and her Romeo.

(Exeunt)

MONTAGUE

I can do you one better! I'mma put up a gold statue of her. As long as people know the name Verona, Juliet's gonna be an icon!

CAPULET

Bet, Romeo will get a statue just as dope! They paid the ultimate price for our beef.

PRINCE

It's a grim morning, folks. Even the sun's too bummed to show. Let's roll and unpack all this. Some folks will get a pass, others will catch heat. Never was there a tale more gut-wrenching than that of Romeo and Juliet.

(And with that, they all head out)

Printed in Great Britain
by Amazon